UNWRAPPED

USA TODAY BESTSELLING AUTHOR
ARIA WYATT

Unwrapped
Copyright © 2023 by Aria Wyatt
www.ariawyatt.com

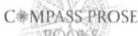

This is a work of fiction. The characters, locations, and events portrayed in this book are products of the author's imagination. Any similarity to real persons, living or dead, or real businesses and locales is purely coincidental and not intended by the author.

Artificial intelligence was NOT used to generate ANY part of this book. *Unwrapped* is entirely a human creation, born from the author's imagination. In addition, no part of this novel may be used as source material for artificial intelligence programs and/or software. Doing so is blatant copyright infringement.

Except for original material written by the author, all song titles mentioned in the novel *Unwrapped* are property of their respective songwriters and copyright holders.

All rights reserved. No part of this book may be reproduced or transmitted in any form or by any means, electronic or mechanical, including photocopying, recording, or by any information storage and retrieval system, without written permission from the publisher at compassprosebooks@gmail.com. Brief quotations may be used in articles or reviews without prior permission. Thank you for respecting the author's intellectual property.

FBI Anti-Piracy Warning: The unauthorized reproduction or distribution of this copyrighted work is illegal. Criminal copyright infringement, including infringement without monetary gain, is investigated by the FBI and is punishable by up to 5 years in prison and a fine of $250,000.

Cover design: Kate Farlow of Y'all. That Graphic.
Editing by Eve Arroyo
Formatting: Champagne Book Design
Paperback ISBN: 978-1-962637-04-6

This book is for anyone stuck going through the motions in a career that drains your soul. I hope you find your passion. And if you do, I hope you hold on to it. Don't be afraid to fill your cup. Spend your days doing something that breathes life back into you.

                    You are worth it.

CONTENT WARNING

Unwrapped contains topics that may be upsetting to readers. Before reading, please review the following list carefully. Feel free to reach out to me via email with any questions that arise. Aria@AriaWyatt.com

Explicit sex scenes & language, including scenes with edging
Brief mentions of historical attempted sexual assault

PLAYLIST FOR *UNWRAPPED*

"Someone Like You" by Adele

"Amber" by 311

"Try" by P!nk

"You Should Be Mine" by 98°

"Giants" by Dermot Kennedy

"Receive" by Alanis Morissette

"So Caught Up" by The Teskey Brothers

"Oh My God" by Adele

"I Want You" by Third Eye Blind

"Not Afraid Anymore" by Halsey

"Movement" by Hozier

"Glow" by Kelly Clarkson & Chris Stapleton

"Fearless" (Taylor's Version) by Taylor Swift

"Lost" by Dermot Kennedy

"No Light, No Light" by Florence + The Machine

"You're the Only Place" by Josh Groban

"It Came Upon a Midnight Clear" by Norah Jones

"Celebrate Me Home" by Josh Groban

"Under My Tree" by *NSYNC

"Underneath the Tree" by Kelly Clarkson

"The Bones" by Maren Morris & Hozier

It was supposed to be a relaxing winter retreat. Except my friends failed to mention the hot doctor I loved in college would *also* be staying at the cabin we rented.

Dr. Dean West broke my heart, but I never forgot him. Not even when I dated his twin brother. Despite the years of distance, our chemistry burns hotter than ever. So do our reasons for staying apart.

When a blizzard snows us in, I discover he's not the same mild-mannered man I knew in college. No, the naughty stranger who ties me to his bed *isn't* afraid of taking what he wants. But I need more. I want our relationship tied up in a pretty bow. But not every girl gets what she wants for Christmas.

UNWRAPPED

CHAPTER ONE

Camille Monet

Mood Music: "Someone Like You" by Adele

MUCH LIKE A WELL-FITTING BRA, ROAD TRIP SNACKS are a necessity. I'm not talking about bottled water and granola bars, either. Who wants flavorless beverages and boring grains when there are tons of more palatable options?

Like coffee and cupcakes, for instance.

Lena Hamilton, my friend and colleague, yanks the passenger door open. "Here. Take these before I spill them." She's balancing two to-go cups and a white box full of decadent treats from Compass Roasters, a coffee shop and gourmet bakery near Manhattan's Bryant Park. She insisted we stop for refreshments before hitting the road, but had I known she would come out with an armload of stuff, I would've gone inside with her instead of waiting at the curb.

I grab the coffees and set them in the center console. "I'm

impressed with your carrying skills," I tease, taking the box so she can get settled. "You sure you weren't a waitress in a past life?"

"Oh, hell no. I'm super clumsy. I'd probably dump people's drinks on their heads." Snorting a laugh, she slides into her seat, closes the door, and clicks her seatbelt. "I'm not kidding, Cami," she reaches for the box, smiling when I hand it over, "these are the *best* cupcakes you'll ever eat."

"My standards aren't high. I mean, as long as there's frosting, I'm happy." I point to her lap. "Why'd they give you such a huge box? Did you buy out the place or something?"

Mischief dances in her jade green eyes. "No comment."

"Seriously, how many are in there?"

Lena grins as she pulls on her sunglasses. "Well, it's a long ride, and I wanted you to get the full Compass Roasters experience, so I may or may not have bought one of each flavor."

I raise an eyebrow. "As in?"

"Fourteen."

"You do realize this bed and breakfast is only two hours away?"

"Your point?"

"I said we needed road *snacks*, not a fourteen-course meal."

Lena caresses the lid. "Girl, you know how I feel about desserts."

She takes them very, *very* seriously.

"True, but—"

"Besides, variety is the spice of life and whatnot." She pulls out her lip gloss and smooths it on. "Whatever we don't finish, we can share with your friends. It's a win-win."

We're traveling upstate to the Mid-Hudson Valley for a long overdue reunion with my pharmacy school roommates.

I've been out of college for a decade. Even though I don't

see my crew as often as I'd like, we're just as close as when we all lived together. We try to meet as a group at least once annually, but there's always someone missing, thanks to our chaotic schedules. This is the first time in three years all six of us will be together. Thanks to the flu, I was the one absent from last year's gathering. Up until a few days ago, I didn't think I'd get to attend this year either, but I finally convinced one of my grumpy coworkers to swap weekends with me.

I ease my Volkswagen into traffic and head for the highway. "Did you pack everything I told you to bring?"

"Yup. I'll have you know, I bought snow pants just for this trip."

Most of us wound up in New York City or the Hudson Valley, so we alternate between the two locales for our gatherings. We try to hit the ski slopes whenever we meet upstate.

"Perfect."

Lena chews her lower lip. "Are you *sure* your friends are OK with me tagging along?"

"Absolutely. They're the definition of welcoming and a blast to hang out with. You'll feel right at home, I promise."

She's a trauma nurse at New York General Hospital where I work as a staff pharmacist. We hit it off the moment we met, and I'm lucky to call her a friend. I know my old roomies will love her. I'm excited to introduce everyone.

"OK, good. I wouldn't wanna interrupt any pill-counting races, or whatever the hell you guys do for fun."

I laugh, knowing the only pharmacists she's encountered are the middle-aged dudes at our hospital with *zero* personality. "Trust me, my friends are nothing like Bob, Hugh, or the rest of the fuddy-duddies I'm stuck with. We're pretty chill. You'll see."

"Jesus. This place is huge," Lena marvels, eyeing the massive log cabin we pulled up alongside. "Wait. Did that sign say it's a vineyard too?"

"Yeah, Queen Bee Bed and Breakfast is affiliated with Boss Bitch Vineyard. Jordana and Talia graduated high school with the woman who owns the whole compound. She always rents us the entire bed and breakfast, so we don't have to worry about disturbing other guests." I flash her a wink. "Because it gets kinda rowdy when we play spin-the-mortar-and-pestle."

She cackles a laugh. "What about seven minutes in heaven? Is there a pharmy version of that? Or do you guys just lock yourselves in people's bathrooms and scavenge the medicine cabinets for expired drugs?"

"I can't speak for the other girls, but I can assure you I've never experienced anything remotely sexual with any of the guys you'll meet. I mean, don't get me wrong—they're all gorgeous, but it's totally platonic. Also, I check expiration dates on everything. I can't help it." It's part of the reason I take forever to do my grocery shopping.

"I know. I saw you in my pantry. I bet you were pissed you didn't find anything."

"Crestfallen. Ruined my whole day."

She giggles and gestures to the parked cars lining the circular driveway. "Looks like a full house."

"Told you there were a bunch of us." I scan the vehicles, recognizing most of them, but there's an unfamiliar black SUV parked between Jude's and Hudson's cars. Maybe one of the girls bought a new ride. I cut the engine and unfasten my seatbelt, pointing to the box of cupcakes. "Let's go in. I'm starving."

We shared a mango treat on our way up the Thruway, but it proved a messy endeavor. Lena wasn't kidding—it was beyond delicious. I've been salivating to try the other flavors.

Frigid air blasts us as we climb from my powder blue Beetle.

Lena shudders. "As my grandmother would always say, 'It's colder than a witch's tit in a brass bra.'" Laughing, she motions to her chest. "Can you imagine if we actually had to wear metal ones?"

"Oh, hell no. I'd go braless."

"Girl, same."

Hustling to the back of my little car, I pop the trunk open to retrieve our bags. Lena's red duffel feels like it's loaded with bricks. "Woman, what the hell did you pack?" I say with a dramatic groan.

Taking it from me, she loops the strap over her shoulder and winces beneath the bag's weight. "Oh, you know, just some books. There's a new Kristie Wolf novel that came out on Tuesday. I'm dying to read it."

It's an understatement to call her an avid reader. She could devour a novel a day if her schedule allowed. I wish I had that kind of attention span. My job saps up what little focus I have, leaving my brain in squirrel mode on my days off, if you can even call them that. My time away from work is hardly relaxing, thanks to a never-ending to-do list. No matter how hard I try to accomplish everything, there are always a few straggling tasks that slide onto the next day's list as little reminders of my failures.

Lena winces again, making me wonder why she bothers lugging around so many paperbacks. "Didn't Marc buy you a Kindle?"

Her future husband is an orthopedic surgeon who works at

our hospital. He's out of town for yet another medical conference. She seemed bummed to spend the week alone—again—this close to Christmas, so I invited her to join me on my venture upstate.

"Yeah, but it's not the same. I need the physicality of a book." She wiggles her fingers. "It's a tactile thing."

"Lemme guess. You're one of those paperback sniffers?"

She snorts. "I don't *intentionally* sniff them, but I do love the smell. Speaking of books, how is yours coming along?"

Writing is the only activity that calms my overactive brain. It's also the most challenging hobby I've ever attempted. I've been *trying* to write a book for years but keep psyching myself out. The writer's block I've been dealing with for the past six months hasn't helped.

"Eh. There are some words," I mutter with a shrug. "They're all shitty, but whatever."

"I'd be happy to read what you've written and give constructive feedback."

The thought of someone actually reading my musings makes me want to vomit. "Maybe someday." I grab our purses and hang my computer bag over my shoulder. "I brought my laptop in case I get inspired. Who knows? The cabin may be the change of scenery I've been waiting for." Hope flickers to life with the idea of progress. Maybe my neglected manuscript will get some much-needed attention. After all, my to-do lists didn't follow me upstate.

"I believe in you, chicky."

"Thanks." *At least someone does.* Nope. Not going there. I'm not ruining my mood with thoughts of my asshole ex. He held the role of mood-ruiner for eight long years.

Lena carries her bag, the cupcakes, and our empty coffee cups as we head for the cabin.

The front door swings open, and my friend Sawyer appears,

wearing an ear-to-ear grin. "Cami, hey! We weren't sure what time to expect you. Let me help you ladies with your bags." He bounds down the steps and rushes along the front path to us.

"Lena, this handsome fella is Sawyer O'Sullivan, aka Sully, and he's the supervising pharmacist at Compass Rose Apothecary in Brooklyn. He and the other guys lived on our floor."

"Hi, Lena." He reaches for our duffels and the box of cupcakes, eyeing her curiously. "You look really familiar. I feel like we've met."

She hands them over with a smile. "We have. You gave me my flu shot in October."

He snaps his fingers. "I remember now. You're a nurse, right?"

"Yes." She glances at me and explains, "Compass Rose has been my pharmacy for years."

"Guess you won't have to worry about not knowing anyone," I tease, nudging her. I turn back to Sawyer. "Are your girls inside?"

Pain flashes across his face at the mention of his wife and daughter. "Uh, no. It's just me this time. Sandra and I are separated now. I'm fighting for full custody. My mother has Kerrigan this weekend."

My jaw drops open. "Oh my God. I had no idea."

Those were the last words I expected to hear leaving his lips. He and Sandra were high school sweethearts. I always considered them soul mates and wished for their kind of bond. I want to ask what happened to tear them apart—and made him pursue full custody of their only child—but now isn't the time.

I grip his arm, peering up at his face. "Are you OK?"

"Not really." He shrugs and meets my gaze, his piercing blue eyes lacking their usual vibrance. "But I'm ... surviving, I guess. The whole situation's a fucking disaster. I'll fill you in later." He points to the front door. "Let's go in. It's freezing."

Lena and I exchange a glance as we follow him inside. My

heart aches for my sweet friend and his little girl. I feel like a jerk for not reaching out more often. I've been so disconnected these past few years. It's a wonder my friends still love me.

The aroma of warm apples and cinnamon greets us when we enter the foyer. Christmas music is blasting, and the cabin's decorations could be featured in a magazine.

"Wow," Lena murmurs. "That tree is gorgeous, and it smells like heaven in here."

"Our friend Jordana has been making pies all morning," Sawyer explains, setting our bags on a nearby bench. "She started with pumpkin. Then moved onto pecan. She's doing apple now. This was *after* the gingerbread and sugar cookies. She said something about Santa's thumbprint cookies too."

I nudge Lena. "Jordy *also* doesn't fuck around when it comes to desserts."

"Uh, clearly. Maybe we didn't need all those cupcakes we brought."

Sawyer laughs. "Don't worry. They'll get eaten. Our buddy Hudson's a bottomless pit," he pats his stomach, "and I'm in a drown-my-sorrows-in-booze-and-sugar kind of mood." He meets my gaze. "Big Shot brought the good stuff."

"I'd expect nothing less."

"Just wait until you see it all."

As CEO of Polaris Drugs, a huge pharmacy technology corporation, our friend Jude Holland is filthy rich. As in, a literal billionaire. He always brings the finest whiskeys and wine vintages to our gatherings. Even though he's rolling in cash, he's still as down-to-earth as when we survived on Ramen noodles and cereal. His generosity knows no bounds. Jude paid off everyone's student loans with his first multi-million-dollar deal, a move that brought me to tears. I'm incredibly proud of his success, and I can't wait to hug him.

I squeeze Sawyer's shoulder. "Wanna share a commiserative drink later?"

"Absofuckinglutely."

Lena and I step out of our snow boots and hang our parkas on the antique coat rack, then follow Sawyer toward the kitchen.

He stops short in the doorway, making me collide with his muscular back. "Holy shit. I was gone three minutes. What the hell happened?"

I step around him to see what he's talking about, then immediately regret it.

Jude and Jordana are crowded around Hudson, who's seated on a stool, his white shirt spattered with blood.

"Keep pressure on it," Jordana commands, wrapping Hudson's hand in a dish towel.

"I'm fine, guys. Everyone needs to chill."

"You're not fine," Jude barks, throwing his hands in the air. "The tip of your fucking finger is missing."

My stomach lurches, and my prickling scalp tells me I'm entering the danger zone. Sweat coats my body in an instant.

Lena rushes over to my friends and leaps into action. "I'm a nurse." She gestures to the freezer. "I need ice. Where's the severed tip?"

"Here." Jordana retrieves something fleshy from the counter and hands it over.

I cover my mouth to stifle a gag and try to force myself to breathe.

Sawyer yanks the freezer open and grabs an ice cube tray, twisting it to free the cubes. Meanwhile, I'm rooted to the floor, blinking rapidly as my vision gets hazy and begins to tunnel. I know I need to sit down, but the scene has me paralyzed with shock and panic.

Thundering footsteps sound from the staircase beside me, and Talia bursts into the room with a dark-haired guy carrying a bag. "Beep, beep. Coming through."

My heart skips a beat when I recognize the one man with the power to break me.

CHAPTER TWO

Dean West

Mood Music: "Amber" by 311

GOOD THING BLOOD AND GUTS ARE MY SPECIALTY. Although I was kinda hoping to escape that part of my life for a few days. Of course, leave it to Hudson to make things interesting. I've known him since college, and he was the catalyst for my decision to pursue emergency medicine. I've been at the bed and breakfast for all of twenty minutes, and the moron has already injured himself. I was upstairs, getting settled in my room, when Talia barged in to announce he'd sliced his finger chopping apples.

Who the hell had the brilliant idea to let him use a knife in the first place?

Hudson Pierce is the reason I keep my medical bag stocked with surgical supplies and bring it literally *everywhere*. This isn't the first time I've had to stitch him up—probably the fourth—and I'm sure it won't be the last. No joke, the guy is a walking, talking, accident waiting to happen. I honestly don't know how he got through organic chemistry without blowing up the lab.

"Excuse me." I brush past the woman in the kitchen doorway and cross the room to my friends, plopping my bag on the counter. "Really, man?"

"It's not like I did it on purpose," he mutters, rubbing the back of his neck with his uninjured hand. "I just wanted to help Jordy with the pies."

Jordana pinches the bridge of her nose. "And I told *you* I had everything under control. Like always, you ignored me and did what you wanted instead. I swear, you'd die if you didn't go out of your way to piss me off."

Grinning, he gives her his good hand's middle finger.

She rolls her eyes. "Right back atcha."

Ignoring their trademark bickering, I shove my sleeves up and quickly wash my hands, then snatch some paper towels before gesturing to Hudson. "What've we got?"

"He's a bleeder, but it's not as severe as it looks," announces an unfamiliar caramel-haired woman who's applying pressure to the wound. "The nail bed is intact. It's just a chunk of the fleshy underside that's missing. Nothing a few sutures can't fix."

"Dean's an ER doctor," Sawyer informs her. He glances up at me. "Lena is a trauma nurse, which is pretty fucking convenient right now."

"Excellent." I motion to my friends. "Can you back up and give us some space please? I don't need you guys up my ass while I suture him."

A loud thud turns everyone's attention to the doorway. The woman I'd passed on my way into the room is now crumpled on the floor. My mouth drops open as recognition slams me in the solar plexus. It's not just any woman—it's Camille Monet, the girl I've been in love with since college.

My twin brother's ex-girlfriend.

"Fuck. I forgot Cami passes out at the sight of blood." Talia's voice jolts me out of my stupor. "Vasovagal syncope or whatever the hell it's called."

I remember my dickhead brother once mentioned her history of fainting, and I know all about the neurocardiac phenomenon from medical school, but I've never seen it happen. I was in such a rush to get to Hudson; I didn't even look at her on my way in. Now I'm kicking myself for the hyperfocus that's both a blessing and a curse. Had I known *she* was the one standing there, I could've anticipated her loss of consciousness and ordered her to sit on the floor with her head between her knees. I could've acted instead of *re*acted.

It shouldn't surprise me—I've been a minute too late my whole life. Especially where Camille is concerned.

"Did anyone see if she hit her head?" I yank the smelling salts from my bag as a chorus of "I don't know" fills the room. Great. The weekend just started, and we've already got a lacerated fingertip and potential concussion on our hands. "You got Hudson?" I ask Lena, relieved to have someone here who's more capable of handling an injury than my crew of pharmacist friends.

"Yeah." She nods. "Go do your thing."

Sawyer follows as I hustle over to Camille and drop to my knees beside her. Everyone else is trapped in limbo, unsure which friend needs their attention more. Hudson's situation might be more urgent, but I can't stop myself from focusing on the raven-haired beauty in front of me.

The girl who got away.

My medical school in Albany was across the street from the college of pharmacy. Since our library was much bigger than theirs, the pharmacy students often studied for exams alongside us. I met Sawyer, Talia, Jordana, Jude, Hudson, and Camille on a stormy Friday night while cramming for my Anatomy and Physiology midterm. They were freaking out over a Pharmacogenetics exam worth fifty percent of their grade. The seven of us hit it off instantly, and we became inseparable. I lived in an apartment across town with my twin at the time. Ryan attended Albany Law School, which is right next to the pharmacy college, so it wasn't long before he infiltrated my new group of friends.

And stole the woman of my dreams.

"Sorry I didn't give you the heads-up she'd be here," Sawyer murmurs, meeting my gaze sheepishly. "But I only found out last night, and I knew you wouldn't come if I told you."

He's the only one I've ever confided in about my feelings for Camille. He knows how it killed me when Ryan swept her off her feet before I had the balls to tell her how I felt. Of course, none of that matters anymore. My brother's betrayal broke her heart. She hates me by association. Now, the relaxing weekend escape I've been looking forward to for weeks, is going to be a tension-filled nightmare.

The invisible band around my chest tightens. "You're right, but you should've told me anyway. Keeping it from me was a dick move."

I should just leave.

Actually, that's perfect. Why ruin Camille's weekend too? As soon as I make sure everyone's OK, I'm out of here. There's a huge snowstorm coming, but I should be able to make it back to Boston before dark. Hopefully. I glance out the window at the darkening skies.

Wonderful. It's already flurrying.

"You're on my shitlist, Sully," I mumble, knowing damn well I'm stuck here.

"I know. I'm sorry, dude."

"Whatever." I brush the hair back from Camille's clammy forehead, then find her carotid pulse, my fingertips pressing into the groove of her slender neck. Her heartbeat thrums a slow, weak rhythm against my fingers, making my heart hammer my ribcage.

Talia approaches with a wet towel and hands it to me. "She's white as a ghost. Is she OK?"

"Yeah." I gently pry open Camille's eyelids to reveal her dilated pupils, then dab at her face with the towel. "Her physical appearance is consistent with a fainting spell, but I can't rule out a concussion." I open the ampule of smelling salts and wave it beneath her nose.

Camille reflexively jerks her head back. Her eyes fly open, and she scrunches up her face at the ammonia fumes irritating her nasal membranes. She blinks up at me, pain twisting her expression. "Ryan?"

I open and close my mouth but can't answer, courtesy of the cleaver in my chest. We may have the same DNA—and an unfortunate resemblance—but I'm nothing like the bastard I shared a womb with. *I* would never have hurt her.

"No, it's Dean," Talia says, squatting beside me. "Do you honestly think we'd invite that pompous dickwad?" She glances at my face. "No offense."

"None taken."

"What's going on?" Camille whispers.

Talia cups her cheek. "You fainted, honey."

"I know. I mean, is Hudson OK?"

"All good over here, Cami-Cam. I'm pretty sure I'll live. It's just a scratch. Dean's gonna stitch—"

"Did you hit your head?" Sawyer holds up a hand to silence him before he says something about blood.

"I-I don't think so."

She tries to sit up, but I stop her with a hand on her shoulder. "Take it easy. It's too soon."

Camille's beautiful green eyes lock with mine and narrow. "I'm fine."

"My medical degree tells me you're not ready to stand up just yet."

"Don't mansplain me," she snaps, fire flashing in her eyes. "Your medical degree doesn't know how I feel on the inside."

Her words go straight to my dick. No, I don't know what she feels like inside, but I've spent *years* fantasizing about it. Even when she was my brother's woman.

"You're right. I don't." I press my fingertips to her neck once more. Her heart is racing now. "But I can only imagine."

A blush crawls up her cheeks when she realizes what she said. "I meant—"

Sawyer clears his throat, glancing between us awkwardly. "Let's get you upstairs, Cami."

I meet his gaze. "She's not ready to walk." The aftereffects of a syncope event can linger for thirty minutes or more. The last thing I need is her falling down a flight of stairs.

"I can walk just fine, thank you." She sits up with a defiance that's nothing short of sexy, then blinks rapidly, like her vision's tunneling again. "See? I'm perfectly normal."

"I'm sure you are." Sawyer wraps his arm around her back and slides the other beneath her knees, lifting her as he stands. "But I'm still gonna carry you."

Camille meets my gaze over his shoulder as they leave the kitchen, her eyes swirling with a thousand emotions. I don't know what stories my face is telling, but the ones written on her features break my heart. Anger mixes with pain and the familiar longing I'd sensed back in college but was too stupid to do anything about.

I stare after them and rub the back of my neck, both concerned about her well-being, and more than a little jealous Sawyer gets to have her in his arms. Things would be so different if my twenty-three-year-old self hadn't been a coward. My mind has replayed that night in the parking lot for the past eleven years. I hate how I clammed up when she put her hands on my chest and leaned in to kiss me. Shocked by the idea of her wanting me, and terrified of ruining our close friendship, I pulled away like a fucking idiot.

I will never forget the hurt in her eyes. The embarrassment and shame. Instead of coming to my senses and going after her, I did nothing. Ryan asked her out a week later. He spent eight years with the woman who should have been mine and callously broke her heart in the end.

"Hey, Doc. You gonna stare into space or suture this finger?" Lena's voice jolts me from my painful reverie.

"Yeah. Sorry. I'm coming." I make my way over and point to the ceiling, once again thankful for the presence of a nurse. "Can you please monitor Camille for concussion signs and symptoms?"

"Sure thing."

"Her heart rate was normalizing, and she denied head trauma, but she's always been stubborn."

Lena snorts. "You think?"

"I doubt she'd tell me if there was an ice pick in her skull," I mutter, gesturing to the counter. "There's a BP cuff in my bag. Take whatever you need."

"On it." Lena releases Hudson and retrieves a few items from my bag before leaving the room.

Feeling the weight of my friends' gazes, I wait until she's

out of earshot before speaking. "Let me guess. Every one of you assholes knew she'd be here but didn't think to warn me."

"We wanted to see you, man," Hudson says.

"Well, you saw me. As soon as everyone's good, I'm gonna head out." Camille's reaction to me resurrected my original escape plan. The kindest course of action—for everyone—involves placing immediate distance between us.

Jordana tugs the straps of her reindeer-covered Christmas apron. "You can't leave. I made pies."

I drag my hand down my face. "Sorry, Jordy, you know I love your baking, but I don't want to ruin everyone's weekend."

"You aren't ruining anything," Talia chimes in, touching my shoulder. "We want both of you here."

"Thanks, but I'm going to hit the road before the snow starts to stick. Then I'll make it back home before dark."

"You're not going anywhere," Jordana snaps, her eyes welling with tears. "Bad things happen in threes. Idiot Hudson cut himself and then Cami fainted. I won't let something happen to you just because your dumb ass wants to drive home in a blizzard to avoid an uncomfortable situation." She snatches my keys from my bag and pockets them. "I'm not fucking around, Dean. Don't make me pop your tires."

"I see you're still superstitious," I say, fighting the smile that wants to break free. She has always been the protective mama bear of our group.

"Damn right, I am."

Talia pours a glass of water and hands it to me. "Relax. It's been three years since they split. She's gotta be over him by now." She cocks her head to the side. "What's he driving these days?"

"Who, Ryan?" I ask after I finish chugging the water.

"Yeah." Talia's eyes have their usual mischievous gleam

when she adds, "Maybe we'll take a ride up to Albany and pop *his* tires for good measure. You with me, Jordy?"

Jordana opens a drawer and pulls out two skewers and a butcher knife. "Pick your poison."

The Maverick sisters have always had my back. I know they'd gleefully slash my brother's tires and key his car if I encouraged it. While I'd never condone vandalism, the pain I saw in Camille's eyes makes me consider giving them the green light.

I set down my empty glass. "I love you guys."

"We love you too," Talia insists, motioning to herself, her sister, and the rest of our friends. "So cut your shit."

"Fine. I'll stay." A sigh heaves from my chest. "But that doesn't change the fact that Camille hates me by association. Don't blame me if the whole weekend is awkward as fuck."

"She doesn't hate you," Jordana soothes, abandoning her weaponry to stroke my arm like she's petting a lion. As the touchy-feely one of our group, she's always hugging everyone and kissing our cheeks. No joke, affection flows out of her in rivers. Except when it comes to Hudson. There's a tense undercurrent there that has never made sense to me. Sometimes I wonder if either of them remembers why they clash. She smiles up at me and ruffles my hair. "No one could *ever* hate you."

"You keep forgetting how different you and Ryan are," Hudson says, slowly shaking his head. "You may share a last name and some gene code, but that's where the similarities end. There's a reason none of us keep in touch with him—he's a dick."

"Besides," Jude's deep voice fills the room as he swirls the whiskey in his tumbler for a few moments. He always does his billionaire dramatic pause when he wants someone's full attention for whatever he's about to say. "You aren't responsible for your brother's actions."

"Thank you." Talia claps his shoulder. "Say it again for the people in the back. Louder this time because Dean's a little thickheaded."

"I mean it." Jude takes a long sip of his booze and pins me with a hard stare. "You need to stop punishing yourself for what he did. I mean, you and Cami were so close back in school. There's no reason his actions should keep you from having a friendship with her."

"Maybe someday." I glance at Talia. "Next time you go to Albany, take a ride down State Street. He drives the gaudy red Mercedes SUV with the SENATOR4U license plate."

She curls her lip. "He *would* have corny-ass personalized plates."

"They're a new development." I roll my eyes. "He got them when he decided on a career upgrade."

"You mean from state Senate to US Senate?" Hudson asks.

"Yeah."

"Cocky prick should've waited until *after* the election," Jordana muses, turning toward the oven to silence its timer. She shoves her hand into an oven mitt. "Everyone, back up so I can get these pies out without burning somebody."

Jude and Talia move to the other side of the island while I turn my focus to Hudson's finger.

"Does it hurt?" Unwrapping the towel, I inspect the wound.

"I mean, it doesn't tickle, but I've been in worse pain." He juts his chin toward his hand. "Can you reattach the skin flap?"

"Yeah, but I don't have anything other than ice to numb you while I do it."

"Wouldn't be the first time."

Ever the smartass, Talia slides a dish rag across the countertop. "You want a towel to bite like they do in the movies?"

He squares his shoulders. "Nah. I can handle it."

While I admire his pain tolerance, the kitchen isn't exactly sterile, and I don't want him to get an infection. Sepsis would really put a damper on our festivities.

I glance at Talia. "Who's working at your store today? I'm gonna phone in some antibiotics and see what local anesthetics you have in stock."

Talia and Jordana own Maverick Fountain Pharmacy, a local, independent drugstore only a few miles from the bed and breakfast.

"Summer's there with Corinne, the student. You probably won't find what you're looking for—a lot of the lidocaine products have been on backorder. Our wholesaler is allocating them because the hospitals need them more." Talia grabs her phone and dials. "So, I recommend you call in something for pain." She hands it over.

I rest the device against my shoulder and continue gathering supplies while it rings.

"I don't need pain meds," Hudson protests, scowling.

Jordana glares in his direction. "And *we* don't need to listen to you whining later when your macho adrenaline has worn off."

The technician answers and transfers my call to the pharmacist on duty. Jordana and Hudson continue to bicker while the others clean up the kitchen, erasing all evidence of his accident.

After I finish calling in the prescriptions, I end the call and hand the phone back to Talia. "OK, you were right. You don't have any locals in stock. We should probably go to the ER—"

"I don't need a hospital. Just do it here." Hudson points to my bag. "You have all your shit with you."

"You realize you'll feel everything, right?"

"You say it like you haven't stitched me up before. I can handle it."

"I'll remind you of that when you start to cry." I turn to the others. "Summer said they're slammed right now, so she'll try to have everything ready in an hour. Someone can go pick them up while I do this stubborn fuck's sutures."

Jude pulls his keys out of his pocket and points to the foyer. "I'll drive. I want to check out the renovations you girls did."

"Wait until you see the soda fountain," Jordana squeals, rubbing her hands together. "The contractors restored everything. It's so perfect—authentic down to the tiniest detail."

He grins. "As if you'd have it any other way."

Talia chuckles. "She's not kidding. The signage, retro bar stools, and the whole vibe of the room make you feel like you've stepped back in time. Jordy designed the menu and bakes most of the goodies you'll see. I keep telling our parents they should've encouraged the pastry chef thing instead of forcing her into pharmacy school."

"Jordy showed them, didn't she?" Hudson muses. "Now they've got the best of both worlds in one kickass establishment."

Jordana eyes him like his praise unnerves her. "You're just saying that, so I keep giving you free food."

"Woman, I'll gladly be your unpaid chore boy as long as you never stop making those brownies."

"I make them for the customers, FYI. Not annoying moochers like you." She turns to Jude. "Tell Summer I said you can have whatever you want from the fountain."

"You might regret saying that." He glances at me. "Is there anything you think I need to pick up for Cami?"

"Uh, no. She should be good." Just the mention of her name makes my groin tighten. "I'll, uh, check on her shortly."

He nods and heads for the front door.

"Good idea." The hint of amusement in Hudson's tone raises my hackles.

"What are you talking about?" I snap, still mildly annoyed by the fact that Sawyer is upstairs taking care of her instead of me. "What's a good idea?"

"I mean checking on the Cam-ster." His lips curve into a grin. "She might need a more *thorough* examination."

I fucking wish. I'd examine every inch of her body if I could.

I clench my jaw instead of answering. I know Sawyer wouldn't open his mouth to the other guys about my feelings for Camille. As much as Hudson plays the jokester hippie card, he's clearly more intuitive than I gave him credit for.

"What's the matter, Dean-o?" he taunts, waggling his eyebrows. "That one hit a little too close to home?"

Talia flicks the back of his head. "He's gonna hit *you* if you don't cut your shit."

Jordana points her peeler at him. "Don't make things any more uncomfortable than they already are. Dean deserves to relax for once." Her eyes meet mine and soften. "And maybe you can try letting things happen instead of fighting them."

"Nothing's going to happen," I mutter, rifling through my medical bag.

"You don't know that." After bleaching the counters and getting clean utensils, she peels a few fresh apples—undeterred by Hudson's bloody setback—and slices them with her usual efficiency, once again demonstrating her baking finesse.

Even though I'm avoiding everyone's gazes, I can still feel

their weight. *They know.* Unease slithers down my spine with the thought. Maybe Sawyer didn't tell them anything, but I'm not fooling anyone when it comes to Camille. There's no other explanation for the matchmaking bullshit they're trying to pull. I don't have the energy to deal with an inevitable rejection, so it's best if I shut them down now.

I spin to face them, crossing my arms over my chest. "Look. I get it. I know what you're trying to do, and I appreciate the thought, but you need to stop."

"We're just try—"

I hold up my hand to silence Talia. "That ship sank before it ever sailed, and I was never the fucking captain in the first place." I shake my head, grinding my molars against the rising tide of bitterness. "And after what Ryan put her through, the *last* person she wants anything to do with is me."

CHAPTER THREE

Camille

Mood Music: "Try" by P!nk

"I'M GOING TO CHECK ON HUDSON." SAWYER PAUSES IN the doorway of the bedroom I'm sharing with Lena and glances at his watch. "We've been up here chatting for almost an hour. Dean *should* be done by now, but I'd rather not take any chances. I'll let you know when it's safe to come downstairs. In the meantime, yell if you need something."

"Thanks," I say, grateful to be in the safety of my room.

"Anytime." He exits into the hallway and closes the door behind him.

Groaning, I squeeze my eyes shut. "Well, *that* was a great start to the weekend."

"Your job right now is to forget everything you saw in that kitchen and relax." Lena settles on the edge of my twin-size bed, where I'm lounging with a stack of pillows elevating my legs. She rests one of her hands on my ankle. "Oh, and maybe explain why Dr. Sexy threw you for such a loop down there."

I knew the question was coming, but it doesn't make it any easier to answer. I can't begin to explain the emotional whirlwind Dean's presence unleashed.

"It's a long story."

She tilts her head to the side. "You didn't mention him when you told me about everyone on the ride up."

"That's because I didn't know he'd be here." I clench my jaw. "Knowing my friends, they kept *that* little detail under wraps for a reason."

"What do you mean?"

"I would've canceled my trip, had I known."

"Why? He seems nice enough."

"Oh, he's very nice. That's the problem."

"Huh?"

"It's complicated."

"I'm listening." Her eyes sparkle with intrigue. "C'mon. Fill a sister in so I don't unknowingly make things worse." The woman should've been a detective because she is relentless in her quest for details.

"I used to have a thing for him back in college."

"A thing?"

"Yeah." A defeated sigh leaves my lips. "Did you ever meet someone and just *click*?"

She nods. "Absolutely."

"Well, that's how it was with Dean. We connected the moment we met and were pretty much inseparable. I mean, we studied together, ate together, grocery shopped together, you name it. I spent more time with him than I did with Talia and Jordana, and I lived with them. He was my rock. I wouldn't have survived pharmacy school without his support." A sharp pang of sadness takes my breath away. Eyes stinging, I stare out the window, needing a moment to recover.

"And?"

I meet Lena's gaze again. "My feelings deepened beyond friendship, and while I thought I sensed an attraction on his end, he made it clear he didn't feel the same way."

"How?"

"He pulled away when I tried to kiss him one night." Echoes of my mortification squeeze my chest. "Lena, I could have *sworn* he wanted me, but I was wrong. I humiliated myself and ruined the friendship. Things between us haven't been the same since."

"Oof. That sucks."

"Yeah," I say lamely, thinking about how I made the shitty situation even worse.

"It's been a decade. You guys can't reconcile?"

"Doubtful. He stopped talking to me after I started dating his twin brother, and, well, you know where *that* relationship got me."

"Holy shit." Her eyes go wide as the pieces fit themselves together. "Senator Douchebag has a *twin*?"

"Yep." I look away and stare at the ceiling fan. "And they're nearly identical, so seeing Dean was a gut punch I didn't need today."

Other than their different eye colors and Dean's height advantage, the men could easily be mistaken for one another. Based on looks alone, that is. Personality-wise? There's no comparison.

"Jesus. No wonder you're off-balance." Lena knows all about my ex's betrayal and the reason I wound up in New York City. She was the first person to befriend me at my new job, back when I was nothing but a shell of myself.

"Off-balance is an understatement." I rub my temples, embarrassed I had to go and faint like some delicate damsel. I'm a medical professional. I should be able to handle the sight of blood. Suppressing a shudder, I meet Lena's gaze again. "And to think I thought I'd be able to decompress up here."

She squeezes my ankle. "I'm sorry, sweetie. Don't worry, I'll do my best to distract you." She grins and gestures to her bag. "Maybe you should read one of my books. I promise there's nothing a giant, fictional cock can't fix."

"I haven't experienced *any* cocks—fictional or otherwise—in three years. I wouldn't know what to do with one."

She cackles. "Oh, c'mon. It's like riding a bike."

A soft knock turns our attention to the door.

I move to get off the bed, but she stops me. "Don't you dare get up just yet." She heads for the door and pulls it open, then immediately stiffens. "Hi. What can I do for you?"

Dean looms in the doorway with his stethoscope around his neck, looking as brutally gorgeous as ever. "I came to check on Camille."

He's one of the few people who use my full name—Ryan always called me Cam—and the way his voice caresses the syllables makes my insides flutter. It's not fair he can still do this to me, even after all the years we haven't spoken.

"She's fine. I'll let you know if anything changes." Lena starts to close the door.

"Wait." He blocks it with his foot and meets my gaze, his vibrant blue eyes searching mine. "I'd, uh, like to check your vitals." He clears his throat. "You know, just to be sure."

Lena peers over her shoulder at me and arches an eyebrow.

"Pretty sure Lena has everything under control, but fine. Do your thing," I mumble, crossing my arms over my breasts. "Wouldn't want to hurt your ego by making you sit this one out."

It's bitchy, but I don't care. How dare he intrude on my reunion getaway. I'm supposed to be relaxing with my friends, not reliving my heartache.

Lena steps aside so he can enter. "She's all yours, Doc."

"Thanks." Regret flashes across his face as he approaches my bedside. He pauses a foot away, tension crackling in the air between us. "How are you feeling?"

"Fine." Other than the fact that I suddenly have difficulty filling my lungs.

"Are you *actually* fine, or are you just saying that, so I'll leave you alone?"

"Both."

"Seems about right." Sighing, he rakes his hand through his thick, dark hair. "I'll make this quick then." He retrieves the blood pressure cuff from where Lena left it on the nightstand. "If I recall, you're a lefty?"

"Yep." I extend my left arm to him, moderately surprised he remembers. "Do you need me to sit up more?"

"No. You're good." He points to my sweater as he places his stethoscope in his ears. "Can you roll up your sleeve though?"

I slide the chunky cable-knit sleeve above my elbow.

Dean settles on the edge of the bed. His warm fingertips brush my skin when he wraps the cuff around my arm and tightens the Velcro. "Too tight?"

"No."

He places the stethoscope's diaphragm over the artery on the inside of my elbow and inflates the cuff. Twisting the knob, he slowly deflates it, listening intently. Once he gets the reading, he releases the pressure and unfastens the Velcro, then returns the cuff to the nightstand. "One-ten over seventy."

"That's typical for—"

His fingertips on my neck steal my words. I know he's only checking my pulse, but I haven't been this close to him since the night I nearly kissed him in college. I force myself to expand my lungs and bury my memories in the past where they belong.

"Your heart's still racing."

You think?

Before I can formulate a comeback, he slides his hands around the back of my neck and gently presses on the base of my skull. "Anything hurt?"

Just my stupid heart.

"No," I croak, forcing the word past my linen throat.

He threads his fingers into my hair and palpates my head. The sensation is almost enough to make me weep with pleasure.

"Any nausea?" His husky voice rumbles down my spine as he continues his examination.

"No." I force another deep breath, which only makes things worse. He's wearing the same cologne he wore in college, and God help me, he smells amazing. My lower belly heats and flutters, telling me I need some distance between us before I get the urge to kiss him again. "This really isn't necessary," I blurt with more snark than intended. Attempting to soften my tone, I add, "I already told you I didn't hit my head."

"Yes, I remember." His amusement-filled eyes meet mine. "But head trauma patients aren't accurate historians, so I'm still going to check for lumps and bumps because I kinda know what I'm doing."

He has no idea what he's doing to my body. Or maybe he does, the bastard.

"Good for you." I avert my gaze and cross my arms again, determined to hide my hardened nipples. Not that he could see them through my sweater, but still. One can never be too careful.

"My expertise is good for *you*, actually." He grips my chin and turns my head to face him, forcing me to look into his soul-stealing blue eyes again. "So how about you keep quiet and let me do my job?"

"Who the hell do you think you are?"

"That's an easy one. I'm Dr. Dean West. I know you hit your head but try to keep up." He snaps his fingers twice.

"I don't like your bedside manner," I snipe, my nostrils flaring. Even though I'm furious, my skin is flushed and tingling, and my panties are damp for the first time in years. It's not fair he can do this to me. "I don't remember you being this cocky."

"I'm not cocky. I'm direct." The hint of a smile plays at the corners of his plush lips. "And you're an uncooperative patient."

"That sounds like a *you* problem."

"Excuse me?"

"It's not my fault you can't handle a simple patient interaction." My smug taunt earns me a glower. Desperate to knock him down a few more pegs and level the theoretical playing field, I add, "I thought communication was the foundation of your profession, Dr. West?"

His eyes burn into mine. "Oh, I communicate just fine, sweetheart." He tightens his grip on my chin and brushes his thumb over my lower lip. "And while I've got plenty of ways to *make* you cooperate, I'd much rather you do it willingly."

Visions of him tying me to the bed flood my mind, stealing what little sanity I have left. I have no idea if he's trying to flirt, but God help me, it's working. I'm ready to strip naked and throw myself at him. He can do an X-ray, CT scan, colonoscopy, I don't give a damn. All I understand is my desire for him. It overpowers logic and reason, which is the only explanation for my next words.

"Maybe I want you to force me."

Dean's sharp inhalation parts his lips, and heat blazes in his eyes as he blinks through his shock. "What?"

"You heard me."

Lena clears her throat. "I'm, uh, gonna head downstairs. It sounds like you two need some priv—"

Dean releases my chin and lurches to his feet, rushing from

the room without another word. The air leaves my lungs when the door clicks shut behind him.

Lena's widened eyes meet mine. "What the ever-loving fuck just happened?"

Good question.

CHAPTER FOUR

Dean

Mood Music: "Giants" by Dermot Kennedy

I don't know if Camille was fucking with me or if she genuinely meant what she said. Either way, I can't stop the lust freight train from barreling into me. My brain taunts me with visions of her on her knees in front of me, those gorgeous pink lips wrapped around my cock, swallowing me down like she's starved for me. Or her beneath me, clawing my back as I thrust inside her. Even better, her delicate wrists tied to the bedpost, holding her in place so I can touch, taste, and fuck her until we don't know our names.

Groaning, I lean against the tile and palm my hard cock. The shower's cool water hasn't done a damn thing to calm my arousal. I need to relieve the tension inside me before I snap, which means I have to rub one out in the middle of the day while my friends are all downstairs. Whatever. It wouldn't be the first time.

I stroke myself from base to tip, rubbing hard and fast, just how I like it. My only goal right now is to come as soon as possible, but if given the chance to be with Camille, I wouldn't rush a damn thing. No, I'd take my time exploring every inch of her body. I'd spend hours kissing and licking her until she was breathless and screaming.

Maybe I want you to force me.

Her words echo in my head as I move. She always had a feisty, take-charge attitude when we were in college. I couldn't imagine her surrendering control to a man—in any capacity—but who knows? Maybe she likes being bossed around in the bedroom. None of my ex-girlfriends wanted any part of my dominant side, so I never had the opportunity to explore the kink I tried so hard to suppress. What if Camille gave me free rein over her body?

I could fuck her the way I always wanted to.

Another groan leaves my chest with the thought, this one rooted in frustration when I remember she hates me. Annoyed with myself for indulging in an impossible fantasy, I tug my dick harder, ready to get this shower jerk-off session done and over with.

Except now I'm more pissed off than horny.

The orgasm that was hovering on the horizon has retreated to the darkened corners of my mind. My thoughts drift to that place where self-loathing and regret run the show, and my hard-on follows, slinking into the shadows like a banished dog.

My passivity is pretty ironic for a man who craves dominance, but it has been that way since birth. I'm forty minutes older than Ryan, born perfectly healthy. He was a different story. When it came time for him to come out, Mom was too exhausted to push. His heart rate kept dropping, so the doctors performed an emergency C-section. Once safely out of the womb, he required a lengthy NICU stay due to underdeveloped lungs.

As the "sick" twin, he needed more care from the jump.

Even after his health improved, he demanded our mother's undivided attention—and received it—while I patiently waited my turn. Our philandering father was never around, and she had *two* infants to care for. As a single mom, struggling to make ends meet, life depleted her energy reserves. Maybe I sensed she was stretched to her limit, or maybe I learned over the years how to make her life easier, but that's what I did.

Our elderly neighbor, Doris, would check in from time to time, lending Mom a hand when she could. When I had lunch with Doris a few years before she passed away, she shared anecdotes from when Ryan and I were little. None of them surprised me—they simply reinforced what I already knew. Doris said I never fussed when I was hungry or tired, content to lay in a soiled diaper until Mom got around to changing me. I didn't complain, whine, or throw tantrums as a toddler. My brother did enough of that.

My own memories from childhood are filled with examples of how I stepped aside for Ryan's benefit. I didn't ask for help with my homework, or ask Mom to play with me, because I didn't want to detract from the little free time she had. I didn't participate in afterschool activities or sports because Ryan already had her running all over town every night for his extracurriculars. I didn't partake in field trips because there was only so much money to go around, and I knew he'd make her feel guilty if he didn't get to go to every single one. Or buy every book he wanted at the Scholastic Book Fairs or get the newest brand-name sneakers.

No, that wasn't me. *I* read the books Ryan lost interest in, dressed in hand-me-downs from our cousin, and wore thrift store shoes. I ate peanut butter and jelly sandwiches every single day because Mom couldn't afford to buy school lunches for both of us. I filled my Christmas list with necessities—like socks and underwear—while Ryan demanded video games. I snuck my weekly allowance back into Mom's wallet, so she'd have money for gas.

I was the boy she called her "strong one." Yes, my health gave me a physical advantage, but it didn't translate into emotional toughness—I still needed love and nurturing, a mother's care and support. But I didn't receive it. Even though Ryan was equally healthy by the time we were two, Mom never got over her fears. She made it my job to look after my brother. Protect him and help him thrive, even at my own expense.

It makes sense I became a doctor—The Dean West default mode is to put everyone else first. Heal and do no harm. Accept and retreat instead of fighting for what I want, need, or deserve.

That's exactly what I did when Ryan pursued Camille. Instead of going after her, I faded into the background. In doing so, I allowed him to hurt her, which is something I'll never forgive myself for.

Sighing, I turn off the water and snag a towel, briskly rubbing it over my body. It doesn't make sense to harp on life's what-ifs or shoulda, coulda, wouldas. I can't change the past. All I can do is plug along in my boring existence and wait for my turn.

But even the strong ones need attention sometimes.

I quickly dress and head downstairs to where everyone's gathered in the kitchen, peering into a big, white box.

Lena points. "If you guys don't mind, I'm gonna snag this one. I've been salivating for it since we left the bakery."

"Go for it," Jude says.

"What kind is it?" Hudson asks.

She holds up an enormous cupcake. "This one's called Caramel Kama Sutra, and it's my absolute favorite. I adore all things caramel."

"Do they all have sexy names?" Talia asks.

Lena nods. "It's Geneva's specialty. Her twin, Lorelei, owns Oral Fixation, a sex-themed dessert bar in this area."

"Oh my God, I love that place," Jordana gushes, snatching a cupcake. "I'm taking the Amaretto Afterglow one. If it's anything like Lorelei's amaretto cookies, I'll be driving down to the city to buy this bakery out."

Sawyer glances at me. "You want a cupcake?"

"Yeah." My stomach growls in support. "What are my options?"

He retrieves a brochure from the box and runs down the list. "Let's see, Strawberry Sex Swing, Cannoli Be You, Chocolate Chip Foreplay, Gimme S'more Lovin', Red Hot Red Velvet, Tie-Me-Up Tiramisu—"

"That one's *mine*." Camille holds out her hand. "Sorry, Dean," her eyes dart to mine for a split second before she accepts the treat from Sawyer, "but the name speaks to me for some reason."

Holy. Fuck.

My dick twitches back to life as images of silk ties and bedposts dance in my head. Forget sugarplums, I'll take blindfolds and handcuffs instead.

Maybe I want you to force me.

Hudson chuckles. "Didn't know you were kinky, Cami-Bear. Or should I call you Madame Monet?"

"No, please don't. It sounds kinda old." She laughs. "And there's a lot you guys don't know about me."

Jordana drapes her arm over my shoulders. "What are you craving?"

"Huh?" I blink, bewildered by Camille's suggestive comments, and more than a little turned-on by the thought of her in cuffs.

Jordana points to the box. "Cami staked her claim. Now it's your turn."

I snatch the list from Sawyer and scan the names. I was too flustered by Camille to pay attention when he read them, but now I know exactly which one I want.

"Well, if I have to choose," I meet Camille's gaze. "Cannoli Be You." Her eyes widen, and she looks away, but I don't miss the faint blush coloring her cheeks.

"Good choice," Lena says, seemingly oblivious to the exchange, even though she definitely picked up on something between us upstairs.

Camille might hate me, but our chemistry is undeniable. What would've happened if Lena left the room and I stayed? I guess I'll never know.

Sawyer hands me the cupcake, which I devour at warp speed. Everyone else makes their selections, and we fall into amicable chatter, catching up on each other's lives.

The fancy gas fireplace gives the cabin's living room a warm glow. We're all relaxing on the couches, digesting the incredible dinner Jordana cooked for us. Hudson just finished telling us about his upcoming trip to Denver to visit his grandmother for Christmas next weekend.

"What are your plans for the holiday, Cami?" Talia asks.

Camille, who's seated on another couch—as far away from me as possible—releases a heavy sigh. "I'm going to a wedding in Manhattan on Christmas Eve. I've been dreading it for months."

"Who's getting married?" Sawyer asks.

"Sara and Drake, people I met through Ryan." Her eyes dart to mine and narrow, then she looks away. Whatever heat I sensed in those green depths earlier has now iced over. "I should've declined the invitation, but Sara's the sweetest human on Earth, and I didn't want to hurt her feelings. She was super supportive after the breakup, and we've stayed in touch."

I've never met Sara, but I know Drake. He's one of my brother's best friends from law school.

Talia curls her lip. "So, wait. Is Senator Dickwad going to be there?"

"He's the best man." Camille twists her hands in her lap. "It's gonna be a rough night for me."

"Can you bring a plus one?" Jordana asks.

"Yeah. I stupidly RSVP'd saying I'd bring someone," she mumbles, gnawing her lower lip. "But I don't have anyone to ask."

If it were any other wedding, I'd volunteer to go as her date, but I can't. Ryan is in the fucking bridal party. The gossip columns would eat that shit up. I can only imagine the headlines. *Senator West's ex-girlfriend has a new man on her arm—his twin brother.* Our mother would chastise me for painting him in a bad light during his campaign. God forbid people see him for the sleazebag he truly is. Then again, going on *any* date with Camille is only a fantasy. I'm the last person she wants to spend time with.

"I'd go with you as moral support, but that's my birthday," Lena says, patting Camille's knee. "I'm hoping Marc will cook a nice dinner for me or something."

"I'll be your wedding date." Jude swirls the whiskey in his glass. "I have nothing going on, and I'll already be in the city later this week."

"Really?" Camille's hopeful expression transforms her features.

"Yeah. If you wanna make the fucker jealous, I'm more than happy to play along."

My chest tightens, wondering how far they'd take their act.

Would he hold her close on the dance floor? Kiss her beautiful lips?

"Oh my God," Jordana gushes, rubbing her hands together. "Cami, it's perfect. You can roll up in one of Jude's fancy cars and march into that wedding with a literal billionaire on your arm. I mean, who *doesn't* want billionaire arm candy?"

"Arm candy? I don't know about *that*." He releases a hearty laugh. "I love you, Jordy. Thanks for stroking my ego." Jude meets Camille's gaze. "She's right about the car part though. Choose whatever one you want to ride in, and we'll take it."

Her eyes light up. "Do you still have the Ferrari?"

"Hell yeah, I do. I also have a Bugatti, a Lamborghini, and a Rolls Royce. As Jordy would say, pick your poison." He rubs his jaw. "What are you wearing?"

"It's a form-fitting red gown."

"Perfect. I'll coordinate my tie with your dress." He sips his drink and adds, "Just so you know, my Bugatti is red. Figured I'd mention that in case you *really* wanna get matchy-matchy."

"The Bugatti it is then," Camille says with a smile. "When I get back home, I'll text you a picture of the invitation, so you have all the details."

"Sounds like a plan, sugar."

Jude was never a fan of Ryan. I'm sure he'd love nothing more than to help Camille make him jealous. The satisfaction on his face makes me suspect his offer goes deeper than that. He's never shown interest in her beyond friendship, but who knows? Maybe I've been too distracted by my own feelings to notice. Balling my fists in my lap, I beat back images of them tangled in his sheets.

"Dean?" Talia tilts her head to the side. "Did you hear me?"

I unclench my jaw enough to speak. "What? No. Sorry. You said something?"

"I asked if you're going to the wedding."

"No. I wasn't invited."

"Don't you guys share a friend group, seeing as you're twins and all? I'd imagine there's some closeness there," Lena says, sipping her white wine. "Or maybe I'm just close with my brother's friends because I like them more than I like him."

"My brother and I have nothing in common. He's a pompous prick who only cares about himself. We aren't close because he lost my respect years ago. I only talk to him to keep our mother off my back." I glance at Camille, hoping she can sense the truth in my words. "We may be twins, but I like to consider myself the better man."

"There's no questioning *that* one," Talia says, elbowing my side. "We know you're a good man, Dean. That's why we keep you around."

Now if only I can convince Camille I'm worth keeping around.

It took me thirty-four years to grow a set of balls. Well, kind of. I doubt the conversation I'm about to attempt qualifies as courage, but it's a step forward for me.

Camille is in the living room, standing near the Christmas tree with her back to me. She's on the phone with the neighbor who's feeding her cats while she's gone. Pausing a few feet away, I wait for her to finish her call. Everyone else is in the kitchen playing Truth Serum, a crazy card game Lena brought, so it's my first opportunity to be alone with Camille.

"I forgot to tell you Nigel only likes the salmon-flavored canned food. Rupert and Alastair will eat whatever you give them." She giggles. "Yeah, I know. They're spoiled, but I love my boys. Give them kisses for me. I really appreciate you, Jen. Thanks. Bye." She slides the phone into her pocket and pivots in my direction, stopping short when she sees me. "Oh, hey. I didn't know you were there."

"I just got here." I clear my throat. "Can we talk?"

She crosses her arms over her chest. "Sure. What's up?"

"I want to apologize to you."

She peers up at me, her eyes narrowing. "For?"

"For what he did."

Camille shakes her head. "You don't need to apologize for his actions. Only he can do that, and I'm not stupid enough to think it'll ever happen."

"You're right. He won't give you that courtesy," I rub the back of my neck, "but I feel like I need to."

"Thanks, I guess." She shrugs.

"I hate that he hurt you."

A humorless laugh leaves her lips. "Hurt doesn't begin to cover it. His affair cost me my dream job, a position I'd worked toward for *years*. Not to mention, I lost my home *and* had to move three hours away to start over. Now I'm stuck in a hospital basement with a bunch of grouchy old men, at a job that sucks my soul. So, yeah, hurt is way too mild a word for what he did to me."

I'll never forget my fury when Talia let it slip that Camille found Ryan in bed with his campaign manager—the night before she was supposed to take her psychiatric pharmacy board certification exam. She was so distraught, she bombed the test, which made her ineligible for the promotion she'd interviewed for.

"I'm sorry on his behalf."

"Don't be. I'm resilient as fuck, and I'm doing just fine without him."

"I'm sure you are, but I'm still sorry you—"

"If you're so intent on apologizing to me, maybe focus on your own actions."

"Huh?" I tilt my head to the side in confusion. "What did I do?"

"What did you do?" Disbelief colors her voice as anger flares in her vivid green gaze. "Oh, I dunno, let's start with how you wrote me off."

"I never wrote—"

"Bullshit," she snaps, jabbing her finger into my chest. "We were so close, Dean. Practically inseparable. You were one of my best friends." Tears fill her eyes. "But you cut me out of your life like I meant nothing to you."

"That's not what happ—"

"Look, I realize I used poor judgment that night in the parking lot, and I'm sorry. I thought I wasn't alone in what I was feeling, but *clearly*, I was wrong." She blinks rapidly and stiffens her spine. "I'm a big girl. I can handle being friend-zoned, but that's not what happened." A tear rolls down her cheek. Then another. She furiously wipes them away. "You stopped being my friend, *period*. You walked away like our friendship meant nothing. My last year of school sucked. You know why?" She doesn't wait for my answer. "I missed our talks. I missed movie night. Taco Tuesday. Our study sessions. I missed those times when we did absolutely nothing, but still had fun together. I missed *you*, Dean."

My chest caves in, learning how much my actions hurt her. "Camille, I—"

"But you didn't care." She steps around me and stalks from the room, taking the steps two at a time.

I stare after her, rooted in place, even after hearing the door to her room slam shut. I kept my distance in the name of self-preservation. I couldn't handle seeing her with Ryan. It ripped me apart, knowing he was the one making her laugh. He got to hold her. Kiss her. Make love to her. He got her time and attention, all because I was too afraid to reach for what I wanted. A coward, like always.

"You OK, man?" Sawyer asks from the living room doorway. He crosses the room when I open and close my mouth a few times, unable to formulate a sentence. "I wasn't eavesdropping, but I overheard most of that," he murmurs, resting his hand on my shoulder. "If you want to talk about it, I'm here."

"Thanks." I force a swallow. "I never imagined my distance would hurt her. I didn't think she wanted my friendship after she got together with him."

"Not everyone is all or nothing, dude. I mean, yeah, maybe she needed a few days to lick her wounds and get over her embarrassment, but she definitely still wanted you in her life." His blue eyes burn into mine. "If you remember, I tried to tell you that."

"I know."

"But you didn't believe me." He shakes his head. "For some stupid fucking reason, you've always had a shitty opinion of yourself. Just because your mom and everyone else around you put that asshole on a pedestal, it doesn't mean he deserved it. And it certainly doesn't mean you should sacrifice your happiness."

"I don't know what to do."

"Well, first you need to figure out what you want," he squeezes my shoulder, "and I think you already know what that is."

I want Camille. In whatever capacity she'll allow. Maybe we can't be together because of her history with Ryan, but I can still be part of her life. I can still be her friend.

"It doesn't have to be all or nothing, dude," Sawyer says, as if he can hear my thoughts.

"How do I get her to forgive me?"

"Communicate. Own up to your feelings and show her you care. Prove how different you are from Ryan. Use actions, instead of empty words."

The problem is, I have no idea what action I'm supposed to take. How do you erase a decade of pain?

CHAPTER FIVE

Camille

Mood Music: "Receive" by Alanis Morissette

My love affair with strong coffee started in pharmacy school. It was the only way I could handle a full day of classes, late-night cramming for exams, *and* my part-time barista gig. While most of my college friends held jobs at local pharmacies, I needed something different. The coffee shop where I worked was a welcoming place with an eclectic clientele that ranged from doctors and lawyers to electricians, mechanics, and artists. I loved watching the creative types who spent their days on one of our stools, sipping java while they worked. I felt at home among them.

I should've taken it as a sign.

While I worked hard for my pharmacist license, my intellectual valor doesn't hold the same weight as it used to. Yes, I'm proud of myself for finishing the program when there were so many times I wanted to quit. The problem is, my perseverance no longer feels like much of an accomplishment. At least, not since the coveted psychiatric pharmacist position slipped through my fingers.

Unlike my friends, my heart isn't in this profession anymore. Pharmacy isn't my calling—it's a job. An obligation. Jude was sweet enough to pay off my loans. While he claimed it was a gift, I feel like a fraud for accepting his money. How selfish would I be to stop practicing when he did that for me? Not to mention, it wouldn't be the first time he came to my rescue.

Shuddering, I push memories of that drunken night back into the darkened corners of my mind. Jude was my literal savior, and I'll forever be thankful for his friendship. Until I have enough money tucked aside to repay him, I'm stuck going through the motions in a career I've grown to hate.

Sighing, I pour myself a cup of coffee, then resettle on the stool at the island. It's three o'clock in the morning. The cabin is silent, save for the gurgling coffee maker. After tossing and turning for hours, I figured I should be productive instead. Books don't write themselves. I need to put in the work, even if it's only a paragraph or two during my early morning writing sprints. I keep telling myself one day things will be different. My unfinished manuscript fills my laptop's screen like the beacon of hope I ache for.

One way or another, I'll make my dream a reality.

For the first time in ages, my fingertips fly over the keys, the words pouring out of me like a waterfall. Last night's run-in with Dean ignited the angsty flame my tears had no hope of dousing. Even now, my eyes still sting from crying myself to sleep.

A noise from overhead makes me perk up. Someone is moving around upstairs, probably making a bathroom trip. I turn my focus back to my words until I hear the stairs creak a few minutes later.

Footsteps approach, pausing in the doorway. "It's the ass crack of dawn. What the hell are you doing?"

I glance over my shoulder at Dean. "Using my laptop."

He chuckles and closes the distance between us. "I can see that." My stomach flutters when he rests his hip against the counter. "I thought the goal this weekend was for everyone to disconnect from work."

"This isn't work." I force myself not to ogle at how sexy he looks in a white T-shirt and pajama pants, his thick hair a tousled mess. "It's for pleasure."

"I think most people's idea of pleasure at three a.m. is vastly different from," he motions to the computer, "whatever it is you're doing."

I shrug and meet his gaze. "What can I say? I guess I'm unique."

His warm smile reaches the corners of his eyes. "That goes without saying."

I give him an exaggerated eyeroll. "Yeah, OK."

His smile fades. "Why are you being so cynical?"

"Don't you know? I'm Camille Monet. It's dictated by my last name."

"Huh?" He frowns and tilts his head to the side.

"I guess you never watched *Clueless*." I release a bitter sigh. "Like a Monet, I'm moderately interesting and appealing from afar, but boring and sloppy up close."

"What the fuck gave you that idea?"

The vehemence in his tone startles me, but I shrug it off. "Your brother. Pretty sure he used those words more than once."

Dean squeezes his eyes shut and clenches his hands into fists. "I know you don't want me apologizing for him, but I'm really sorry he said that. It couldn't be further from the truth." His eyes fly open and burn into mine. "If it wasn't a blizzard out there, I'd drive up to Albany and punch him in the face."

"I appreciate your offer," I touch his muscular forearm, "but he's not worth the assault charge."

"I'm serious, Camille."

When his intense gaze doesn't falter, I shift on my stool. "Thanks, but it's fine. I'm over it."

"Well, I'm not. It'll be a long time before I forget what I just heard."

I sigh and drag a hand over my face. "Listen, I'm sorry. I didn't mean to be so bitter. I slept like shit, and I'm a little cranky."

"Don't worry about it." He points to my computer again. "What are you writing?"

"A book."

My weak admission earns me a nudge. "You say that like it's not the coolest shit ever."

"Well, it's been a struggle."

"Why?"

"Aside from my usual lack of focus, I've kinda had writer's block." Sure, I've been adding words to my document, but I haven't truly connected with them. Or much of anything else in my life.

"How come?"

"Because writing is personal, and it's really fucking scary to pour your soul into something."

"I'm sure it is, but you've always been brave." He pulls out another stool and settles beside me. "Tell me more."

"What do you want to know?" I ask, equal parts warmed and confused. Brave is the last adjective I'd use to describe myself, but it feels good knowing he thinks of me that way. Ryan never wanted to hear about my story. He thought my time would be better spent advancing my career, instead of having my *head in the clouds, chasing a childish dream.* Funny how he's the one who cost me the credentials I tried to add after my name.

"What's the premise? Is it fiction or nonfiction? What inspired you to write? Tell me everything." Genuine interest shines in his deep blue eyes.

I hesitate for a moment, unsure if I'm ready to be vulnerable this early in the morning. Then again, he witnessed my meltdown last night, so it's not like I have an image to uphold.

"It's fiction," I finally murmur, fiddling with my necklace.

He smirks. "That's pretty broad. Can you maybe narrow it down a little?"

My cheeks heat. "Well, um, it's a love story."

"Nice." He gives an appreciative nod. "Everyone enjoys a good happy ending. Or at least *I* do."

"Oh, I bet you do." I laugh and gently shove his shoulder. "Pervert."

Chuckling, he holds up his hands in surrender. "For once my pun *wasn't* intended."

"I'm truly shocked."

"No, really. I didn't realize how it sounded until it came out, but it made you smile so I don't regret saying it." He scoots his stool closer. "Tell me about your characters."

I launch into a full description of my pharmacist heroine, complete with her demographics, physical traits, wounds, quirks, and goals. Dean listens intently, nodding and smiling at my level of detail.

"So, what are the tropes?"

"Listen to you, Mr. Romance Book Expert."

He laughs. "Hey, now. Sometimes I know things about stuff."

"To answer your question, it's what they call a second-chance romance. As I said, the heroine is a bit of a dreamer. She sees the beauty in life and the good in people—even when they don't deserve it."

"Kinda like you," he murmurs, rubbing his jaw thoughtfully. "No matter how stressed you were in school, you always stopped to appreciate the little things. Like that time we went to the Tulip Festival. Remember how hard it rained?"

"We were drenched," I agree with a smile.

"But even so, you didn't get pissed off, or run toward the car like we'd melt. Instead, you admired the way the raindrops clung to each flower. You stared at Washington Park like it was the most beautiful place you'd ever seen and told me it reminded you of a misty day in Ireland. You said the weather made you want to sit in front of a fireplace in a thatched-roof cottage and drink herbal teas. Then we went to your job—soaking wet—to have chai lattes and cinnamon biscotti."

I blink a few times and stare at his face, shocked he remembers that day with such vivid detail. And that he picked up on the fact that I based the heroine on myself. Here I thought I was being stealthy.

"What?" He squeezes my knee like he always did back in school, and it sends a flare of heat between my thighs. "Did you think I'd forget?"

"No, um. I guess I'm surprised you're able to quote something I said eleven years ago."

"I've got plenty of your quotes in my Camille cache. As you mentioned last night, we were pretty much inseparable." Clenching his jaw, he closes his eyes for a moment. Regret glows in his gaze when he reopens them. "I'm really sorry for hurting you. I swear it was never my intention."

I want to ask him what he thought would happen when he cut ties, but that would lead to more tears. I've already cried enough on this trip.

"Thank you," I whisper, as the invisible band around my chest tightens and my eyes start to burn in warning.

Once upon a time, he was my best friend. Now we're strangers dancing around our history.

"I mean it." He brushes his thumb over my knee, and we sit in silence for a few beats. "So, tell me about your hero." When I give him a puzzled look, he adds, "The guy in your story."

"Oh, um . . ." Panic flares in my gut when I realize he's about to figure out my inspiration for the heroine's love interest. "He's, uh, a bit of a cinnamon roll."

"A what?"

"He's one of the good guys." *Like you.* Minus the whole vanishing from my life part, obviously. My subconscious is quick to remind me of my own missteps, and I cringe.

Noticing my discomfort, Dean pins his gaze to mine. "You give me the girl's entire life story, but when I ask about the dude you compare him to a pastry?" He nudges my arm. "C'mon. You gotta give me more than that. What are his core wounds or whatever you called them?"

"He's too focused."

"OK, now we're getting somewhere. What does he do for a living?"

Oh, fuck. "He's . . . in the medical field."

"Perfect. You know all about that. I imagine it's easier to write what you know." He places his elbows on the counter and rests his chin in his hands. "OK, so, medical field. Is he a pharmacist too?"

"No."

"A dentist then?"

"No, he's—"

"A nurse? An optometrist? A proctologist?"

I giggle despite my rising panic, hiding my face in my hands instead of answering.

"You're really not gonna tell me?"

I peer between my fingers at him. "He's a doctor."

"Nice. What kind of doctor?"

Deciding there's no way I can humiliate myself worse than when I tried to unsuccessfully kiss him, I drop my hands into my lap. I stiffen my spine and look him square in the eye. "Doctor Sean East practices emergency medicine. He's emotionally unavailable and hates praise. He enjoys single-malt scotch, baked potatoes, and a good steak. He's afraid of moths, slugs, snails, eels, and swimming in lakes and ponds—the latter two, courtesy of his fear of leeches. He's also well aware his distaste for slimy things makes *zero* sense, given his chosen profession. But that's another story. Anyway, his mother neglected him, so he never learned to appreciate his worth. He has a shitty habit of putting himself last. Anything else you'd like to know?"

An electric current charges the air between us as realization kicks in. Dean stares at my face but doesn't speak, his shoulders rising and falling faster than before. I hold my breath, waiting for him to retreat like he did in college, but he doesn't move.

"I have another question," he finally says, his deep voice rumbling down my spine. "What does he look like?"

"Use your imagination."

His gaze darts from my eyes to my lips, then back again. "For the record, I'm not afraid of moths. Their powdery wings gross me out. It's a texture thing—the same reason I hate chalk."

"Would you let a moth crawl on you?"

"Fuck no."

"Then you're afraid of them," I announce smugly.

"We'll have to agree to disagree." He twists my stool so I'm facing him head-on. "But I do agree with something you said last night."

"And what's that?"

"I owe you an apology. If I could go back in time, there are a lot of things I'd do differently."

"Like what?"

"Just about everything." He cups my jaw with both hands. "Since I'm a doctor, I'd triage my fuckups in order of importance and address the most critical mistake first."

"And that was?" My shallow breaths give the question a wispy tone, like wind rustling through tall grasses.

He brushes his lips over the shell of my ear and whispers, "Not doing *this*."

I can hardly breathe when Dean presses a kiss to my cheek. My jawline. My neck.

As much as I want to grab both sides of his face and swallow his tongue, I wait. I made my move eleven years ago. Now it's his turn. The desire burning inside me drowns out the little voice reminding me of my history with his brother, and the fact that he lives in Boston. Associations and distance don't matter. All that exists in this moment is the sensation of his warm lips peppering kisses on my throat.

"Jesus, Camille." Lifting his head, he rests his forehead against mine, breathing just as heavily as I am. My heart beats even faster. He pulls back to meet my gaze, stroking his thumbs over my cheeks. "You should have been *mine*."

"You didn't want that."

"*Yes*. I. Fucking. Did." His nostrils flare with the growled confession.

"Then why'd you push me away?"

"I panicked that night because I was afraid to ruin our friendship, but that's exactly what happened. By the time I got the balls to confess my feelings, it was too late." Fire blazes in his eyes. "I wanted you then, and I want you now. Nothing has changed for me. I kept my distance because I couldn't handle seeing you with him. It broke me apart." He swallows and rubs the back of his neck.

"Why didn't you say something?" I whisper, blinking my emotions away before they spill over.

"Because you'd moved on, and I wanted you to be happy."

"I didn't move on. I wasn't happy. It was a lie I told myself to deal with your rejection." I clutch his shoulders, remembering my juvenile attempt to distract myself with another guy. His twin brother of all people. *How could I have been so stupid?*

"Camille, I—" He squeezes his eyes shut and tries again. "I'm so sorry."

"The truth is, he was a shitty substitute. Those eight years were a cruel imitation of what could have been. No matter how much I tried to convince myself he was the next best thing, his behavior highlighted your differences. I *knew* he was wrong for me—you two are nothing alike—but I was really fucking lonely." I swipe at an escaped tear. "I settled when I should have waited. And look where that got me."

He meets my gaze, and the raw emotion in his eyes cracks my chest wide open. "You're breaking my heart."

"Well, it's true. He wasn't you, Dean. He could *never* be you."

"You're right. He couldn't." He grips my shoulders and crushes his mouth to mine, seizing my lips in a bruising kiss.

Kind, gentle, cinnamon roll Dean morphs into an alpha male right before my eyes. He shows me no mercy, holding me in place while he takes what he wants. I kiss him back just as hard, moaning when he yanks me into his lap. I knot my fingers in his hair and wrap my legs around him.

Fueled by regret, misinterpretations, and wasted time, it's a kiss to end all kisses. He urgently slides his tongue against mine and tugs me deeper into his lap. A groan leaves his chest when I grind against his hard cock and tug his hair.

He grabs a fistful of my ass and breaks the kiss. "You keep rolling those hips and I'm gonna fuck you."

"Maybe that's what I want."

"I'll give you anything you want, sweetheart." He kisses me again, deeper this time, like he's pouring his soul into me.

"Need you," I whimper, dragging my hand down his chest.

He lifts me onto the countertop without breaking the kiss and stands between my parted legs. Just as he's about to slide his hand beneath my nightshirt, Hudson walks into the room.

CHAPTER SIX

Dean

Mood Music: "So Caught Up" by The Teskey Brothers

CAMILLE YELPS AND PULLS AWAY FROM ME AS HUDSON wordlessly saunters through the kitchen. He opens and closes a few random cabinets and drawers, then opens the oven, seemingly oblivious to our presence. Hopefully he doesn't notice the hard-on tenting my pajama pants.

"What are you looking for, Pierce?" I say, walking over to him.

He doesn't answer, just continues staring into the empty oven.

Camille hops down from the counter and approaches with a worried look on her face. "Are you OK, Hudson?"

He straightens and ambles past her, opening the walk-in pantry. "I've been looking for you. Let's talk business," he commands, addressing a few cereal boxes and cans of soup. Then he steps inside—without turning on the light—and closes the door behind him like it's a private office.

Her brows knit together. "What the hell's wrong with him?"

"You want a list?"

"I'm serious, Dean. He's acting weird."

"He's fine." I stare at the door, half expecting him to jump out and scare us like a demented jack-in-the-box. "He's sleepwalking."

Of all the people in this house, accident prone Hudson has to be the one who sleepwalks? This has disaster written all over it. My boner decides to call it a day, deflating like a sad balloon.

"What should we do?" She smooths her hair and fixes her shirt.

"Nothing. When he comes out of there, I'll walk him back upstairs, so he doesn't hurt hims—"

Something crashes inside the closet, followed by a thud. Camille's widened gaze snaps to mine.

"Son of a bitch." I rush over and yank the door open.

Hudson's sprawled on his back. The shelf that once held canisters of uncooked pasta is now on the floor beside him with all its contents. I can't help but chuckle at the sight of him covered in macaroni and broken lasagna noodles, holding an open canister of rigatoni like a football.

My presence seems to register because he asks, "Why'd he hit me?"

"No one hit you, man."

"He shoved me off the barstool."

"You were sleepwalking," Camille says softly, stooping to retrieve the canister he's holding.

He hugs it to his chest. "No, no. I need this for the plants."

"Holy shit, I think he's still asleep." She presses the back of her hand to his forehead. "He doesn't feel like he's burning up or anything."

The noise roused someone else—or several someones—because now there are footsteps coming down the stairs.

Jude rushes into the room, followed by Jordana. "What was that crash?"

"Is everyone OK?" Jordana stops short beside me, her eyes widening when she spots Hudson. "Oh my God, what happened?"

"Quiet," Camille says, holding her finger to her lips. "He's still asleep."

Jude's eyes dart from the spilled pasta littering the pantry to the open oven. "Please tell me he wasn't trying to cook."

I rub the back of my neck. "I have no clue what his plans were, but he's lucky he didn't set the place on fire."

"Or fall down the fucking stairs," Jordana hisses, wringing her hands. "He's not even awake, and the moron is *still* causing problems."

Jude scans the kitchen. "What time is it? Should I run to Walmart and pick up a baby gate or something?"

I shake my head. "Nah, then he'll just hit it with his knees and fall face first down the stairs."

"Good point." He props his hands on his hips like a construction site foreman assessing his workers' progress. "So, what should we do with him?"

Hudson rolls to his side, resting his face on his bicep. He's still snuggling the metal canister, but his eyes have drifted closed.

"Let him sleep," I say with a shrug. "If falling didn't wake him, we won't be able to do it without freaking him out."

"You think?" Jude asks.

"Yeah, he'll probably be disoriented, and I'm not in the mood to get punched in the face."

"I'm curious to hear his dreamland version of what happened." He nods to the pasta. "Not gonna lie, it's kinda funny."

Camille swats his arm. "Don't make fun of him. He could've gotten hurt."

"I'm not making fun of him, Cami. I just find it comical he's on the floor in a closet, spooning a canister of spiral noodles, with fucking orzo in his hair. It's the kind of shit that would only happen to him."

She smirks. "Good point."

Jordana gestures to Hudson. "Someone take a picture so we can show him when he wakes. Knowing him, he'll find it hilarious." She rubs her hands up and down her bare arms. "It's freezing in here. I'm going to get him a blanket." She heads for the living room.

"He probably won't remember any of this," I tell Jude.

"You and Sawyer never mentioned him sleepwalking back in school," Camille says, peering up at him.

"I honestly don't think he did. I mean, *I* never saw or heard anything, but I'll ask Sully in the morning."

Jordana returns with a blanket and decorative throw pillow. Her feet crunch on pasta as she shoves the pillow under Hudson's head and unceremoniously drapes the fleece over him. Exiting the pantry, she addresses Camille and me, "How'd you two get down here so fast?"

Camille's eyes widen for a moment before she regains her composure. "Oh, um, I was already awake, working on my laptop." She gestures to me and flushes when I give her a secret smile. "Dean came downstairs for a glass of water. We were chatting when Hudson strolled in."

Good save.

"Actually, I got up to use the bathroom, but came downstairs to investigate when I smelled coffee. Given the inhumane hour, I figured maybe we had a domestic poltergeist. But lo and behold, *someone* is moonlighting as an author. Did anyone else know Camille's writing a book?"

Jordana rubs her hands together. "Oh my God, you're finally doing it?"

Camille flushes an even deeper shade of pink. "Yeah, kinda." Her eyes dart to mine. "But I wasn't ready to broadcast that yet."

I tilt my head to the side. "Why not? You should be proud."

"Well, for starters, I'm an *aspiring* author—not a real author."

"Nope. None of that negativity." I pin her with a hard stare. "You're writing. That makes you an author. Don't discredit yourself."

My tone leaves no room for rebuttal, but this is Camille. Naturally, she has another argument.

"Thanks, but it feels too weird saying that when I'm not convinced it's a done deal. I mean, I have a *long* way to go before this book is finished."

"You'll get it done. I believe in you." Motioning to our friends, I add, "We *all* do."

"Dean's right. We believe in you. Besides, we're your best friends. We're supposed to know this kind of shit," Jordana chides, settling on a stool. "Now that we've got that cleared up, tell me *everything*."

Jude squeezes Camille's shoulder. "I think it's cool as fuck, Cami. I can't wait to hear all about your book. But first, coffee." He crosses the room and pulls a mug from the cabinet. "Anyone else need some?"

"Me please." Jordana raises her hand. "Light and sweet, thank you."

"Coming right up. Cami, you need a refill?"

"I'd love one. Thanks."

"You got it, sugar."

Tensing, I stare at Jude's back while he pours coffee for the women. It's now the second time he's called Camille *sugar*, and I don't like it. She's mine. Of course, he doesn't know that yet, but I plan to have a little chat with him later.

"Dean, you want coffee?"

"I'll get some after I shower. Thanks." I need to clear my head and deal with the blue balls situation down yonder.

"Sounds good." He brings their mugs to the island, then grabs his own and takes a long sip, peering at Camille's computer screen over her shoulder. "I want to hear all about this author gig."

"I'll see you guys in a bit," I grumble, annoyed he's standing so close to her. I want to be the one near her.

God help me, I will *never* recover from that kiss. After spending years fantasizing about her—fucking pining—there aren't words to describe how it felt to finally have her in my arms. If Hudson hadn't ruined the moment, I would have been inside her. My dick twitches in agreement.

I head for the staircase, pausing in the kitchen doorway. "Hey, Camille?"

She looks over her shoulder at me. "Yeah?"

"How does the story end?"

Staring into my eyes, Camille ponders the loaded question. "I'm glad you asked," she finally murmurs, and the emotion in her gaze could bring me to my knees. "But I haven't figured that out yet."

CHAPTER SEVEN

Camille

Mood Music: "Oh My God" by Adele

I PEEK OUTSIDE TO WHERE THE GUYS ARE SHOVELING THE front path and cleaning a foot of snow off everyone's cars. "I'll be honest. I'm really not in the mood for skiing."

Lena sets her coffee mug on the nightstand and shrugs. "So don't go."

"But I feel bad ditching you."

"Don't feel bad. It's not your job to entertain me." She moseys over to where I'm standing, wipes steam from a windowpane, and stares outside. "Look at all those men out there exerting themselves. I can't believe they wouldn't let us help." She chuckles and weaves her long hair into a braid. "I mean, I'm not complaining, but I feel a little guilty lounging while they work."

"Same."

My eyes follow Dean as he heaves a shovelful of snow off

the path. I felt his muscles when we kissed, and sweet baby Jesus, the man is a chiseled masterpiece. He's so gorgeous, I find it hard to breathe when I'm around him.

I can't believe I spent eleven years under the impression he wasn't interested in me. If only I'd turned Ryan down when he asked me to attend a concert with him. I was so stupid for allowing my hurt and embarrassment to get in the way of logic. I should've spent more time licking my wounds. Maybe then I wouldn't have allowed someone to give me new ones.

Cringing, I push thoughts of Ryan aside. He doesn't deserve space in my head. Dean, on the other hand, is worth all my brain's real estate. My lower belly flutters, remembering our time in the kitchen. He certainly didn't kiss me like the quiet gentleman I met in college. No, there was nothing gentle about the way he claimed my mouth. Domineering, passionate, and intense, he kissed me like he'd been waiting his whole life to taste my lips.

Lena notices my gaze riveted to Dean and nudges me. "Will I be the only non-pharmacist on the mountain, or is a certain someone going too?"

"I think he's going." I'd filled her in on everything that happened in the kitchen because I needed a sounding board, and I know I can trust her to keep her mouth shut.

"I have an idea." Her eyes sparkle with mischief. "Perhaps you should feign an injury, so the good doctor feels compelled to stay here and take *care* of you." She shimmies her hips in a mini salsa dance. "Are you picking up what I'm putting down?"

I laugh. "I always do."

"It's perfect. I'll go with your friends. That way, I can burn off all the pie and cupcakes I've eaten, stay out of your hair, *and* keep an eye on Hudson, who shouldn't be skiing—or shoveling the damn driveway—in the first place."

"Tell me about it. That man needs a *lot* of eyes on him."

"Seriously. I can't believe he made it down the stairs safely but fell in the pantry." She cocks her head to the side. "Did he ever sleepwalk in college?"

"No."

"Is he under a lot of stress?"

"I'm really not sure." I chew my lip, annoyed with myself for not staying up to date on my friends' lives.

Lena resettles on her bed. "Should I sleep on the couch tonight to give you some privacy?"

I snort a laugh. "I highly doubt anything else will happen. Realistically, we're a bad idea. Aside from the whole ex-boyfriend's twin issue, Dean has a job he loves in Boston. I'm really not interested in doing the long-distance thing. If I'm going to be with somebody, I wanna be *with* them."

"Believe me, I get it," she mutters, twisting the enormous diamond on her finger. "I spend far more time alone than I'd like."

"Hopefully that will change once you guys get married. Have you set a date yet, by the way?"

"No."

I expect her to elaborate, but she stares at her ring in silence. Most newly engaged brides-to-be are more than willing to gush about their wedding plans. Not Lena, apparently. While I don't want to probe, I want to be there for her if she's having a hard time.

I walk over and settle on the bed beside her. "Everything OK?"

"I don't know." Her jade-colored eyes meet mine, and the sadness in them is unmistakable. "Did you ever get a gut feeling?"

Dean stomps snow off his boots and leaves them on the mat inside the foyer. He meets my gaze as he unzips his coat and hangs it on the coat rack. I've been relaxing on the loveseat, enjoying the fire.

He approaches with a smile that heats my insides. "You ready to hit the slopes?"

"Not really."

"How come?" His dark brows come together. "You love to ski."

"I'm just not feeling it."

"Are you OK?" Concern laces his voice as he settles beside me.

"I'm fine. It's just not what I feel like doing."

"What would you rather do?"

You. "Well, I'm feeling inspired, so I wanted to do some writing."

He squeezes my knee. "I meant what I said earlier. I think it's an amazing endeavor, and I'm really proud of you."

His praise warms me. "Thank you."

"Can I ask you something?" He searches my face. "It's kind of personal."

"Go for it."

"Where'd your sudden inspiration come from?"

I lift my chin. "It's not sudden. I've been trying to write this book for ages."

"Right. But you also said you've been dealing with writer's block." He holds up a finger. "Not to mention, you *love* to ski, yet you're ditching a chance to hit the slopes so you can write."

"Is that a crime?"

"Nope. I'm just curious what's fueling your fire."

Heat crawls up my neck and cheeks as my gaze darts from his eyes to his plush, kissable lips. "I think you know the answer to that."

He licks his lips. "Maybe I want to hear you say it."

"Maybe I'm not concerned with what *you* want." My syrupy sweet reply makes him grin.

"How would you react if I decided to skip the mountain today?" he asks, dragging his thumb over my knee in slow circles.

"It's a free country, Dr. West. You do you."

He suddenly stands and brushes imaginary dirt off his jeans. "I think I'm going to hit the shower again, and I dunno, maybe take a nice, long afternoon nap." He pins me with his heated gaze. "If you're in the mood for any more *inspiration*, you know where to find me."

CHAPTER EIGHT

Dean

Mood Music: "I Want You" by Third Eye Blind

I HAD EVERY INTENTION OF GOING SKIING. I REALLY DID. Until I saw the desire in Camille's eyes earlier. Aching for a chance to be alone with her, I told my friends I hurt my back shoveling and needed to skip the slopes. Now I'm lounging on my bed—squeaky clean from the day's second shower—catching up on emails while I wait for them to leave.

I can't get Camille out of my head. While I feel guilty for lying to my friends, I couldn't miss an opportunity to make up for lost time with her. Hopefully, she has something similar in mind. My dick twitches again, all too willing to bring the fantasy to life, but it goes beyond my inner horndog. I need to repair our bond. Camille needs to know how deeply I care. I'm still reeling from learning how much my distance hurt her.

A knock reaches my ears, making me launch myself off the bed. I yank the door open, hoping to see Camille, but it's Hudson.

"Hey, man. What's up?"

He sighs. "Can you please do something about my finger? It's bleeding through the bandage."

Of course it is. The idiot insisted on helping us shovel instead of staying in like I advised.

"Pretty sure we told you we'd handle the driveway."

"I wanted to help."

"I know but ripping out your stitches isn't helpful. Let me wash my hands, and I'll take a look at the damage." I head for the bathroom attached to my room.

"I probably shouldn't ski."

"I told you *that* too," I say over the running water. "Maybe you should start listening to me." Once clean, I rejoin him in the bedroom.

"Yes, Dad." Smirking, he rakes a hand through his hair. "I guess I'll sit this one out."

Great. While I don't want him to hurt himself—again—I was hoping for an empty house for a few hours. Looks like that won't be happening. Which, if I'm being honest with myself, is for the better. I shouldn't start something with Camille. We live in different states, and she's my fucking twin's ex. I can already hear my mother ranting about it. Besides, the last thing I want to do is hurt Camille again when I inevitably disappoint her. She deserves better than me.

I release the world's heaviest sigh. "Good call."

"You OK, man?" Hudson eyes me.

"Never better." I grab my supplies from my medical bag and unwrap the dressing.

"Sorry about wrecking the pantry this morning. And for fucking up my stitches. And for all the other dumb shit I've done."

I chuckle. "Feeling remorseful, are we?"

He shrugs. "Feeling a lot of shit lately."

"Wanna talk about it?"

He shakes his head. "Nah, I'm good. Thanks."

Hudson is the jokester of our group. It's unsettling to see him somewhat somber, but I know him well enough to know he won't talk unless he's ready to.

"I'm here if you change your mind." I quickly clean his wound and use medical glue to close the area where he popped a stitch. Then I bandage him back up.

"Appreciate it, man," he says on his way out the door.

"No problem."

Soon, Sawyer, Jude, Lena, Jordana, and Talia load up someone's SUV and head for the slopes. Still quiet, Hudson settles on a couch to watch soccer, while Camille types away on her laptop in the kitchen. As much as I'd hoped to spend time with her, I don't want to disturb her creative process. So, here I sit, alone in my room with nothing to do.

I was joking when I mentioned the afternoon nap earlier, but now the idea appeals to me. Especially since I slept like shit, and I've been up since three. Yawning, I lower the shades to darken the room. I don't need it pitch-black, but the low winter sun reflecting off the snow is blinding. I strip down to my boxers and a T-shirt and pull the covers back.

Yeah, a nap sounds great.

I close my eyes and allow myself to drift, but just as I start to go under, another knock reaches my ears. Groaning, I toss the blankets off and pad over to the door. I pull it open to find Camille standing in the hallway, looking beautiful in yoga pants and a college hoodie.

Her eyes widen as she takes in my appearance. "Hey. Did I wake you?"

It dawns on me that I'm in my underwear, but it's too late

to do anything about it. Besides, I've never been all that modest to begin with.

I drag a hand through my hair. "No. Just resting my eyes."

"May I come in?"

Fuck yeah, you can. "Sure." I step aside so she can enter.

"I'm tired of looking at my computer. Figured I'd visit you for a change of scenery."

I close the door and turn to face her. "Like what you see?"

I meant it as a joke, but the look in her eyes is far from joking. She drags her heated gaze up and down my body, her shoulders rising and falling faster with each breath.

"Yes," she finally whispers. "Very much so." Her cheeks flush pink as she stares up at me. "But that's nothing new."

Holy fuck.

We stare at one another in silence for what seems like an eternity. I wait, knowing where I want the encounter to lead, but unsure if that's the direction we're heading—even though she's in my bedroom, visibly turned-on.

Finally, my patience wears thin. "We both know you didn't come up here to look."

"You seem so sure of that."

"Am I wrong?" When she doesn't answer, I move closer, so our bodies are inches apart. My cock hardens between us. "What can I do for you, Camille?"

"Yesterday, you said you could force my cooperation." Lifting her chin, she looks directly into my eyes. "Prove it."

CHAPTER NINE

Camille

Mood Music: "Not Afraid Anymore" by Halsey

Shock registers in Dean's eyes for only a split second before the hunger takes over. He backs me to the door, caging me in with his arms. "Say that again."

I hold his gaze with a brazen confidence I didn't know I possessed. Or maybe it's bravado. Who cares? All I know is my desire to lose control. With Dean.

But his hesitance is getting old fast.

"You heard me."

"Say it again," he repeats on a low growl.

"I *said*, I want you to prove your ability to force my cooperation, but since you seem a bit dense, I'll paraphrase. Show me you're capable of taking what you want for once."

"I'm more than capable."

"Prove it then."

"If that's what you want," he pins me against the solid oak

with his hips, and his erection presses into my belly, "you're gonna see a side of me you might not be ready for."

"Trust me, I've been ready for over a decade."

"Oh yeah?" Dipping his head, he brushes his lips over my ear. "Then pick a safe word."

"You're serious?" I gasp as he drags his tongue up the side of my neck.

"You're goddamn right, I am." Pulling back to meet my gaze, he firmly grips my jaw. Fire burns in his eyes. "You want me to take charge?"

"Yes."

"Then pick a fucking word."

I say the first thing that comes to mind. "Politician."

A dangerous smile curves his lips. "Good choice."

"Seemed fitting." Any thoughts of Ryan would surely be an instant buzz kill—for both of us.

"Here's what's going to happen." He jerks his thumb over his shoulder. "You're gonna let me tie you to that bed."

"Oh really?" I raise an eyebrow. "What's your plan after that?"

"I'm gonna fuck you the way I've always wanted to."

Heat floods between my thighs, and my knees buckle, just thinking about it. I never knew this side of Dean existed. With his kind demeanor and gentlemanly ways, I'd always pegged him as passive. I imagined he'd be a tender lover. Clearly, I was wrong. The man before me is nothing like my mild-mannered friend from college who always let me make all the decisions.

Now that I've had a taste of this version of him, I want to see just how dominant he can get. "And how, exactly, do you want to fuck me?"

"Hard and deep. Until there's no question you belong to me." He trails his fingertip down my cheek. "You should have been mine eleven years ago, Camille, but I fucked up. Now I'm gonna fix that." Rolling his hips, he lowers his mouth to my ear again. "Trust me, sweetheart. I'm going to fuck all memory of him out of your head. But I'm warning you—I won't be gentle about it."

"Good. I don't want gentle."

"I won't stop unless you say the word."

Now that he's finally taking what he wants, I never want him to stop. "I won't say it."

"I wouldn't be so sure of that." He crushes his mouth to mine, kissing me with the same brutality as he did earlier.

Weaving my hands into his hair, I give it right back with a desperation born from years of having to settle for less than I deserve. Dean hooks his hands beneath my thighs and lifts, guiding my legs around his waist. His iron length rubs against my pussy as he grinds his hips. The friction curls my toes. I pull his hair. He bites my lower lip, making me gasp.

He stares into my eyes. "You ready for me?"

"Yes. Don't hold back, OK?"

His gaze darkens. "Camille, I've wanted you for so fucking long, I won't be *able* to hold back." He kisses me again, slower and sweeter this time, then carries me over to the bed. He plops me onto the mattress. "Rest your head on the pillows."

I do as I'm told, watching as he crosses the room to retrieve a condom from his bag. Next, he snatches his jeans from a nearby chair and meets my gaze while pulling his belt from the loops. Just when I think things can't get more enticing, he rummages in his medical bag.

"You gonna give me a checkup, Doctor?"

He withdraws his stethoscope instead of answering. Next, he wordlessly locks the door and drags over the desk chair. Tilting it, he wedges the back beneath the doorknob so no one could get in if they wanted to. My heart beats faster with his every move, and despite his obvious arousal, he carries himself with the determination of a king who has all the time in the world to pillage and conquer.

"Take off your hoodie," he commands, approaching the bedside with his belt and stethoscope.

Sitting up, I lift the garment over my head and toss it aside. Beneath it I'm wearing a tank top and bra. I meet his gaze and wait for his next directive. I'm not typically a woman who allows a man to tell me what to do, but Dean's assertiveness is the sexiest thing I've ever encountered. I never envisioned him as a take-charge alpha male, and I certainly never imagined him in a position of sexual dominance. But here he is, making me crave a submission I didn't know *I* was capable of.

"Remove your shirt and bra." He kneels on the edge of the mattress. "Do it slowly."

Gripping the tank top's hem, I leisurely expose my torso. My lace-covered breasts. My collarbone. Once it's off, I throw it by the sweatshirt and turn my attention to my bra. While I love the thought of him ripping my clothes off, there's something empowering about stripping in front of him. I've waited eleven years for this moment. I refuse to rush it. The reverence on his face when he finally sees my naked breasts makes me feel like a goddess.

"So beautiful," he whispers, moving closer to press a kiss to each one. "Lie back for me."

I rest against the pillows once more and peer into his gorgeous, soulful eyes. I'm afraid if I blink this experience won't be real, and I can't bear the thought of reverting to our years of distance. Dean has always held a piece of my heart. I miss being his friend. I want him back in my life, in whatever capacity he'll allow.

"Give me your hands." His roughened voice makes my inner muscles clench.

I hold them out in front of me. Dean grabs my wrists and

lifts my arms over my head. Using his belt, he secures me to the slatted headboard, tightening the length of leather until I gasp.

"Too much?"

"No."

Nodding, he removes his shirt and places the stethoscope around his neck.

Mother of God, the man's body is gorgeous. He's perfection from his well-defined pecs to his chiseled abs. Dark hair coats his chest and trails down his stomach, disappearing beneath his waistband. His hard cock juts against navy-blue boxer briefs.

He stares deep into my eyes. "Tell me your safe word."

"Politician."

"Don't forget it." He grips the waistband of my yoga pants and slowly slides them down over my hips. His fingertips travel my goose bumped legs as he drags the pants to my ankles and tugs them off. Next goes my panties.

"Fuck, you're so beautiful."

"Thank you. You're not too shabby either." I jut my chin toward the belt securing my hands. "What about my ankles? Aren't you gonna tie my feet too?"

"Silly woman," he says, stroking up and down my thighs. "That wouldn't work."

"Why not?"

"Because then I couldn't do *this*." He shoves my legs apart and licks his lips at the sight of me spread open for him. Our eyes meet. Holding my gaze, he lowers himself between my thighs. The wicked smile on his face tells me he'll show no mercy—just like he warned.

I can't breathe, can't think, with his decadent mouth so close to me. "Oh, God."

"I haven't even touched you yet." His low chuckle gusts his warm breath over my skin.

"I know, but it's been a long time since anyone has."

"I'll keep that in mind." He kisses my inner thighs. Slowly. Deliberately. Like he has all the time in the world. Like we haven't waited eleven years for this. He inches closer to my pussy, then moves away, repeating the act until I'm delirious with anticipation.

"Dean, please..."

"Please, what?"

"Put your mouth on me."

"I am, sweetheart." He switches sides, his nose grazing my clit as he moves.

I gasp and buck my hips, but he still holds out on me, raising himself up onto his elbows. Then he flashes me a smile and places the stethoscope in his ears.

"What are you do—"

Dean presses the metal disk to the middle of my chest. "Your heart's racing."

"You think?"

"I wonder what happens when I do this?" He drags the cold metal over my nipples, with that same tortuously slow pace before pressing it above my heart once more. "It's beating even faster now. It sounds like you're out of breath."

"I'm not," I lie, attempting to expand my lungs.

"You sure?" His devilish smile widens before he kisses my lower belly. Keeping the stethoscope's diaphragm in place, he trails his lips toward my pussy. Closer and closer until he's right above my clit. "How about now?"

"*Dean.*" I tilt my hips upward with a whimper.

"I love hearing you say my name even more than listening to your heart race." He flicks and swirls his tongue on my clit for a few seconds. "But I'm gonna make you give me both."

I strain against his belt, desperate to pull him closer.

"Don't bother trying to break free. I'm going to be here a while." He licks up and down my center and groans. "Fuck, you taste like heaven."

All I can do is moan as he teases my body's most sensitive area. He plunges his tongue inside me, like he's known me intimately for years, making me arch off the bed. Refocusing on my clit, he sucks and flicks and swirls until I'm ready to come, then abruptly stops.

"Don't stop," I beg, reeling from the ecstasy and desperate for more.

Rearing up, he removes the stethoscope and places it in my ears. "Listen to your heart race."

"I don't need to hear it. I know it's fucking racing."

"Listen anyway." He holds the diaphragm to my chest and lowers himself between my thighs once more. Instead of resuming with my clit, he eases a long finger inside me.

My heartbeat thunders in my ears. "Dean, *please*."

"Tell me how it feels."

"So good." The words leave my lips on a moan.

Watching his movements, he slowly pumps his finger in and out. "You're soaked, sweetheart." He presses my legs wider apart and adds a second finger, thrusting with the same agonizingly slow pace. "So tight. Can you handle one more?"

"Yes," I whimper.

He slides a third finger inside me, curving them to rub my G-spot. My body clenches around him as he continues to stroke them in and out. Then he mercifully returns his attention to my clit, sealing his mouth over it.

"Oh, yes," I hiss when he gives me a hard suck. My heart thumps its approval. My hips thrust to meet his movements as he unravels me. I dig my heels into the mattress and struggle against the leather binding my wrists. "Dean, your tongue feels so good."

He doubles down on his efforts, groaning when I squeeze his head between my thighs. I'm literally fucking his face now. One more swirling flick, and I'm gone.

I wail his name as I fall apart, writhing on the bed. My pussy spasms around his fingers, but he doesn't stop. He doesn't ease up on my clit either.

"Dean, I can't take—" My second climax steals my words.

He keeps moving like he'll die if he stops. The tension builds and crests in under a minute.

"Oh, God, Dean."

"Give me another," he growls, pulling my body closer to his mouth.

I thrash my legs. "It's too much. I can't—"

"Yes, you can. And you *will*." He holds me in place. "I'm nowhere near finished with you."

Another orgasm seizes me, and I cry out, unable to keep quiet if I tried. Hudson's downstairs, but I stopped caring if he—or anyone else—hears me. I've never orgasmed this many times in a row. I've never had anyone show my body this kind of attention. The pleasure is too much for me to handle.

"I can't take anymore."

Dean sucks my clit harder, making me come *again*. I'm a sweaty, writhing mess and he shows no sign of stopping. My heartbeat echoes over my wailing moans. I'm going to disintegrate. The intensity has moved beyond a level I'm comfortable with.

"You've gotta stop," I plead.

He meets my gaze and raises his eyebrow like I'm supposed to be doing something, but he doesn't stop licking me.

"Dean!"

He raises his head. "Do you want to use your safe word?"

"Not exactly, but I'm getting there. I need things to slow down."

"I can do that." He resumes at a much slower pace, licking and kissing with a gentle tenderness he lacked before, but I'm already too sensitive. My body quivers and clenches as the pleasure coils tighter. Before I can catch my breath, yet another climax rockets through me.

I squeeze his head between my legs. "Politician!"

Dean immediately rises to his knees and reaches for the belt, quickly untying my hands. Massaging my wrists, he stares into my eyes and lowers my stiffened arms. "Are you OK, sweetheart?"

"Yes. No. I don't know."

"You told me to slow down, but now I'm realizing you meant stop." He squeezes his eyes shut. "I fucked up. I'm sorry if that was too much for you."

"It kinda *was*. But it also wasn't. Does that make sense?"

"Surprisingly, yes." He brushes my hair back from my sweaty forehead. "Are you sure you're OK?"

"Yeah. I just need a breather."

"Let me get you some water." He grabs the empty glass from his nightstand and heads for the bathroom.

I'm sprawled on the bed like a limp noodle, completely spent, pulsing with the aftershocks of my orgasms. I've never experienced anything like that. After three years of celibacy, I was afraid my body wouldn't remember how to respond. It turns out I had nothing to worry about.

Dean once again proved he's nothing like his brother. We didn't even go all the way, but the encounter was more intimate than anything I shared with Ryan. My ex was lazy in bed. He wanted me to do the work—strip for him, suck his dick, ride him. Our sex life always felt like a performance. Since he cheated, I assumed he lost interest in what I had to offer.

It was refreshing to have someone else run the show. To have a man lavish pleasure on me, instead of expecting me to simply get him off.

Dean returns with water and a wet cloth. He gently wipes my face, then presses it between my thighs before helping me sit up. "Drink," he commands.

I chug the cool liquid and set the empty glass on his nightstand. "Thank you."

"My pleasure."

"Speaking of," I motion to his dick, "I'm sorry I had to tap out before you got yours."

He settles on the bed and pulls me close. "Trust me, I'm more than satisfied."

"But we didn't—"

"Watching you unravel was better than any sex I've had." His eyes burn into mine. "And hearing you moan my name was the best gift I've ever gotten, so please don't worry about a damn thing. You were perfect. Better than I *ever* imagined."

"You've imagined me?"

"Sweetheart, you've starred in my fantasies for *years*."

Experiencing true intimacy cracked open the shell around my heart, allowing vulnerability to seep in, which fuels my need for reassurance. "Really?" I whisper, staring into his deep blue depths.

"Yes really. Remember when we crammed for finals at my place? I'm talking about the night with the freak thunderstorm."

"Of course." We lost power, but we were so nervous about our tests, we used flashlights to keep studying.

He runs his fingers through my hair. "You have no idea how badly I wanted you that night. We were on the couch. You were wearing a skirt. All I could think about was how much I wanted to kneel on the floor in front of you, shove your skirt up around your waist and throw your legs over my shoulders."

I flush with the visual. "You were so quiet though."

"Because I was afraid of telling you how much I wanted you. Fuck whatever I was studying, I wanted to learn *you*. Kiss you. Hold you. Touch you. Lick you until you screamed."

"I thought I was the only one having fantasies in the dark."

"Definitely not. I can't tell you how many times my mind has wandered back to that night."

"Mine too. I wanted to kiss you but didn't have the guts to try. Until, well, the night that shall not be named."

Regret burns in his eyes. "I wish I could go back in time and do things differently. I need you to know that, Camille."

"I do, now."

"It fucking kills me that I hurt you." He slowly shakes his head. "I'm sorry for being too young, stupid—and afraid—to act on my feelings." He grips my chin. "I need you to *know* I wanted you all along. Pretty much since the first time we hung out alone."

That's also around the time I started fantasizing about him.

"I had so many chances to make you mine, but I fucked them all up by being a coward."

I'm not about to argue with him on that one, so I keep quiet, peering up into his eyes instead. Now that he's finally expressing himself, I don't ever want him to stop.

"That night, on the couch, I wanted to be inside you more than I wanted to breathe." Kissing my forehead, he adds, "I still do, actually."

"What are you waiting for?"

CHAPTER TEN

Dean

Mood Music: "Movement" by Hozier

"MAKE LOVE TO ME, DEAN."

There aren't words to describe how it feels to hear Camille make the request. Her unwavering gaze tells me she's serious, but I don't want to rush her. She needs time to recover after I pushed her boundaries.

"Are you sure?"

She cups my face. "We're alone for a few more hours. Let's make the most of them."

I seize her lips, pressing her back onto the bed as I lower myself on top of her. The kiss becomes frenzied when she hooks her fingertips in the waistband of my boxer briefs and shoves them down to my thighs. I kick them the rest of the way off.

She wraps one delicate hand around my cock, stroking me from base to head. "My God, you're huge."

"Glad you think so."

Camille tightens her grip, making me groan. It's been a long time since any woman has touched me. I'd forgotten how good it feels to have someone else's hands wrapped around my dick. I snatch the condom from the nightstand and tear open the wrapper. She releases me so I can roll it on.

Hovering above her, I meet her gaze and line us up. "You sure you want this?"

"Yes."

I ease inside her, forcing myself to take things slowly when what I want is to pound her into the bed. She gasps and clutches my back.

"You OK?"

"Uh-huh. It's just been a while, that's all." She clings to me for dear life.

I clench my jaw and sink all the way inside her. "Fuck, you're so tight," I whisper, rocking my hips so she can acclimate. "Tell me to stop if it hurts."

Nodding, she wraps her legs around me and hooks her heels behind my thighs. I kiss her hard and deep, moving my tongue the way I'd love to thrust my cock. Even though I'm dying to fuck her hard, I need to take it easy. The last thing I want to do is hurt her.

I roll my hips and deliver a few short strokes. We both moan when she slides her hands to my ass and pulls me deeper.

"You're killing me, sweetheart. I'm trying to take it slow."

"I don't want slow. Or gentle. Do what you said you'd do and make me forget."

My earlier words echo in my brain. *I'm going to fuck all memory of him out of your head.*

"Like this?" I surge forward and slam into her, making her cry out.

"Oh, God, *yes.*"

Something awakens inside me, a fantasy I've kept buried

for years. One where I'm a man who isn't afraid to take what he wants. I want Camille. All of her. I want her writhing beneath me, moaning and screaming my name. I want her desperate and aching for me. My kiss. My cock.

I *need* her to submit to me.

After spending my entire life in the back seat, I'm finally ready to grab the wheel—even if it's only in bed.

In my mind, I'm not a passive bystander. I'm a goddamn king. A monarch who's waited eleven fucking years to stake his claim.

"Put your arms over your head," I command, rearing up onto my knees. "Spread those pretty thighs for me."

She complies immediately, unleashing my dominant side. Snatching her wrists, I use one hand to pin her to the bed, then grab the back of her leg for leverage and start to move. Her lush tits bounce with every thrust. Next time we get together, I'm going to take my time and suck on those perfect pink nipples. Right now, she wants it rough.

I lose myself in the sensations, sinking my cock into her warm, tight body. I honestly don't think I could slow down if I tried. Her pussy was made for me. It's amazing how much better sex feels when you share a connection with the person you're fucking.

I haven't been with a woman in over a year, and even then, it was a lackluster experience. No one could compare to the fantasies in my head. I tried relationships, but my heart wasn't in it. Come to think of it, my heart has *never* been involved. I guess I've been holding out for the one I truly want. God help me, Camille is everything I imagined and more.

"You feel so fucking good, sweetheart," I say on a groan.

She whimpers my name and arches off the bed. "Oh, God. I'm so close. Please don't stop."

Keeping my gaze locked on her face, I move even faster. The headboard slams the wall with each thrust.

"Come for me." I growl the command. She feels so incredible, I don't know how much longer I'll be able to last. I've ached for this woman for years, and to finally have her in my arms is a gift I never thought I'd receive.

She wails my name and comes on my cock, her gaze never leaving mine. Releasing her hands, I lean over her, deepening my thrusts to meet her bucking hips. She rakes her nails down my back and squeezes my ass.

"That's it, baby. Pull me deep."

Camille digs her nails into my ass cheeks. "Kiss me."

I crush my lips to hers. Tongues dancing, we kiss like we're starved for each other. She tightens her legs around me. My hips move on their own, driving my cock inside her with hard, deep thrusts.

She breaks the kiss. "It's always been you, Dean."

Me. She wants me.

Her confession sends me over the edge. My body goes rigid, and a guttural groan leaves my chest as I come. Shockwaves of pleasure radiate from my dick to my toes, and I've never felt a release so sweet. It goes on for what seems like an eternity, until I'm finally spent.

Gasping, I rest my forehead against hers. "You all right?"

"Yes. You?" She's still clutching me like she's worried I'll levitate away from her.

"God, yes. Camille, I—" *I've always loved you. Let's spend the rest of our lives together.* I swallow and try again. "I don't have the words." Pulling out, I roll to my back and tug her close, kicking myself for not revealing my truth. "You're perfect." *Perfect for me.*

She rests her head on my shoulder, her fingertips tracing the ridges of my abdomen. "You're really good in bed."

"Uh, thanks." I chuckle and kiss the top of her head. "Likewise."

"I loved seeing that side of you."

We lie in silence for several minutes as our breathing and heartrates even out. She feels so right in my arms. I don't know how I survived a decade without her. Now that I've felt her soft, warm body pressed to mine, I never want to let her go.

"Do you tie up all your women?"

I tilt her chin to make her meet my gaze. "I don't have other women. I haven't been with anyone in over a year."

"But did you tie her up?" She wrinkles her nose, like the thought of me with another woman disgusts her.

"No. I've never done it before."

Her eyes widen. "Seriously?"

"Yeah."

"But you seemed so . . . comfortable taking charge like that."

"Probably because it's been a fantasy of mine since college."

"Tell me more."

"Whenever we'd hang out together, whether it be to study, or for one of our other adventures, I never wanted it to end. There were so many nights when you were packing up your books to go home . . ." I clear my throat and release a heavy exhale as the memories come flooding back.

She feathers her fingertips over my pecs, toying with my chest hair. "Keep going."

"I hated when you'd leave."

"Me too."

"I used to envision tying you to my bed so I could make you stay."

"I would've stayed if you asked me."

"That's the thing. I never had the balls. Believe me, there were so many times I spent hours trying to work up the courage, but I couldn't do it. Then, I'd mope around the apartment after you left."

She reaches up to stroke my cheek. "Sounds like you were just as lonely and miserable as I was back then."

"Yeah." I meet her gaze. "So, to answer your question, no. It never crossed my mind to tie up another woman. You're the only one I've ever wanted to keep."

"I wish you'd tried harder to keep me." Her eyes mist over, and she blinks rapidly to clear them.

"Me too, sweetheart. I'm so fucking sorry I let you go." My chest tightens. "I caused us both so much pain. I'd give *anything* to go back and fix it." The gravelly tone leaving my lips doesn't even sound like my voice, probably because my remorse makes it hard to breathe, let alone speak.

"And I wish I hadn't been so stupid." She squeezes her eyes shut. "I'm sorry I hurt you by being with him. I didn't know how you felt."

I brush my thumb over her lower lip. "That's because I didn't tell you. I walked away when I should've fought. We wasted so much time." I pull her closer, like my hug can erase the painful years that passed.

"How do we navigate all this going forward?" Her voice is soft, uncertain.

Good question. The fact remains we live in different states, and she's my twin's ex. My mother will disown me if I tarnish the golden child's image during his campaign. Despite Ryan's shitty character, he's still my brother. It's my job to help him succeed.

I clench my jaw, knowing this is the same thought process that made me lose her eleven years ago. The problem is, I'm not sure how to move beyond it. My chest tightens even more with the realization I'm at risk of seeing history repeat itself. "We'll figure it out."

We have to. How? I'm not sure, but I owe it to both of us to try.

Hudson doesn't make eye contact when he enters the kitchen, just makes a beeline for the fridge.

"You hungry again?"

"Nope." He withdraws a beer and cracks it open, then leans against the counter and chugs the entire thing like he used to do in college. Crushing the empty can, he finally meets my gaze. "Thirsty."

"Are you OK?" Camille walks over to him.

He lifts an eyebrow. "Are *you*?"

"Why wouldn't I be?"

"Good point." Hudson smirks and holds her gaze. "Interesting choice in safe words, Cami-Cam."

Her cheeks flush pink. "I don't know what you're talking about."

"Uh-huh." He points toward the living room. "I'm not sure what kind of duct system they typically have in log cabins, but there's like a vent or whatever in the ceiling over the couch."

He heard everything.

Camille opens and closes her mouth as her cheeks turn an even deeper shade of red.

He rubs his jaw. "Politician is a good one. I mean, I probably would've chosen organic chemistry, myself. Fuck that shit, am I right?" He glances at me. "So, did the headboard damage the wall?"

I cross my arms over my chest and shoot him a glare instead of answering. Camille hides her face in her hands, clearly embarrassed. I'm not the slightest bit ashamed of what happened. I am, however, annoyed he overheard us. Her moans are for my ears only.

He motions between us. "So, you guys are a thing now?"

I step closer to him. "Do you have a problem with that?"

"Of course not." His gaze locks on to mine. "But I can think of a few people who will."

CHAPTER ELEVEN

Camille

Mood Music: "Fearless" (Taylor's version) by Taylor Swift

"Do you think I'm a shitty person?" I gnaw my lower lip and glance at Lena, who's seated on the edge of her bed, towel-drying her hair.

She flips her wet tresses back and meets my gaze. "Absolutely not. You're both single, consenting adults. What you do behind closed doors is your business."

"Unless someone overhears the entire thing."

Mortified, I retreated to my room after the Hudson encounter. Dean wanted to come with me, but I told him I needed time to think. I dozed off, exhausted from our vigorous sex, and more than a little emotionally drained. I'm not sure how long I slept, but I didn't wake until Lena came into the room after everyone got back from the slopes. Of course, she *immediately* knew something was wrong and dragged it out of me in typical Lena fashion.

"Well, there's *that*." She laughs. "But I don't think Hudson's the type to spread shit around. I mean, I just met him, but he seems like a good guy."

"True." Sighing, I flop back onto my bed. "But what about Ryan?"

"What about him?"

"They're family. *Twins*, Lena."

"Listen to me. That man cheated on you and caused you to fail your board exam. You don't owe him any courtesy."

"I know, but I just don't want to cause any problems for Dean."

"Well, realistically, there *will* be some fallout. You need to prepare yourself for that, but you should also remember his family ties are not your problem. It's something *he* needs to come to terms with." Her eyes meet mine. "If he's a smart man, he won't walk away from you again."

"He lives in Boston," I whisper, wrapping my arms around myself in a hug.

"Would you ever consider moving?"

"I don't know." I hug myself tighter. "I mean, I already started over three years ago. Yeah, my job sucks my soul, but I'm finally making friends and feeling at home in my apartment."

"Maybe try the long-distance thing?"

"But then we can't, you know, *be* together."

"Does your bond go deeper than sex?"

"Absolutely." At least it *did*, back when we were friends in college. Now, I'm not so sure. We've only been reunited for one day. It will take much more than that to erase a decade of hurt.

She sets her towel aside with a shrug. "Then you find a way to make it work."

"Yeah," I say lamely, as doubts and fears swirl in my head. "How do you and Marc keep things exciting with him traveling so much?"

"Please don't use us as an example."

I tilt my head to the side at her hollow tone. "But you've been together a few years, and now you're engaged—"

"We haven't had sex in close to a year." She stares at her ring sadly.

"Seriously?"

"Yup." She squeezes her eyes shut. "Believe me, it's not for a lack of trying—on *my* part, anyway. Marc just isn't that into me."

"But he asked you to marry him last month."

A humorless laugh leaves her lips. "That's what successful surgeons do, right? They find themselves a little nurse wife who's totally cool with spending the rest of her life as an afterthought."

Holy shit.

The sadness in her eyes takes my breath away. "Lena, I—"

"I'll be fine." She plasters on a weak smile. "Enough about my situation. Let's focus on you."

While I'm sure she changed the subject for a reason, I want her to know I care. "If you ever need someone to talk to, I'm here."

"Thank you. I appreciate that." She waves a finger at me. "Just promise me you won't make my mistakes." Her eyes burn into mine. "Demand respect, and for the love of all that's holy, *don't* settle for less than you deserve. If Dean is someone who fills your heart—without sex—keep him. But if sex is the only thing that ties you, cut him loose. Because, believe me, once the sex stops, all you'll have to fall back on is your friendship." She twists her ring in circles. "If that's not there, then you really don't have anything."

Lena's words have echoed in my mind all evening. The poignancy behind her message struck a chord, making me reflect on the past decade of my life. Ryan and I weren't friends. Our hot and heavy relationship started on a whim, all because of my wounded pride. While we shared some fun times, my hollow happiness didn't feed my soul.

Dean, on the other hand, fortified me. Once, he made me banana muffins as a reward for acing one of my midterms. He mistakenly used salt instead of sugar, and while they tasted truly awful, I ate every single one. I didn't have the heart to tell him how gross they were. He figured it out when he tried one of his creations and immediately spit it into a napkin. When it came time to celebrate the next exam, he hit up a local bakery and purchased a cake.

I could be myself with Dean. He didn't care if I hung out in pajama pants and a hoodie. He didn't give me shit for stress-eating. He never made fun of me when I cried during sappy movies. He let me try to teach him the choreography I'd memorized as a teenage *NSYNC fan. We shopped. We hiked. We played in the snow.

Dean made me feel whole.

While I'd give anything to throw myself into his arms, I need to remember we went over a decade without speaking. We went from best friends to literal strangers. Sure, I attended his med school graduation—with Ryan—and kept tabs on him over the years, but I'll never forget how much he hurt me when he wrote off our friendship.

I've grown a lot since college. My dreams and goals have changed. He doesn't know the person I've become.

"You OK?" Talia hands me a wet plate. We volunteered for cleanup duty after dinner.

I dry the plate with a dish towel. "Yeah. I took a late nap. I'm a little out of sorts." I'm not ready to delve into whatever is happening with Dean, so I change the subject. "How was skiing?"

"Awesome. I rode the lift with Sully a few times. We had a heart-to-heart. Has he told you any details about the separation?"

"No, only that it happened. He seemed miserable when he mentioned it, so I haven't brought it up."

She sighs heavily. "It's bad, Cami. I'm worried about him. He's going to need our support. I don't know how he's going to—" Movement over my shoulder catches her attention. "Hey, Dean."

"Hey. You ladies need any help?" He comes up beside me, and my insides flutter with his sudden closeness.

Talia flashes him a grin. "Way to wait until we're almost done. Thanks though."

"Sorry. Jordy had my ear about the pharmacy renovations." He touches my arm. "Can I talk to you?"

"Sure." I set the plate and towel on the counter before following him out of the kitchen.

He leads us into the cabin's dining room, which is empty now that everyone is lounging on the couches with full bellies.

Pausing beside Christmas tree number two—the place has four—he turns to face me. "You're upset." His concerned gaze meets mine. "Please talk to me."

"I'm not upset." I wrap my arms around myself in a hug.

"You've barely said two words to me in hours. I know you're avoiding me."

Here I thought I was successful in not making it obvious.

I stare at a sparkly reindeer ornament, admiring this tree's woodland theme. "I guess I'm a little overwhelmed maybe. And confused."

His fingertips brush my chin as he gently turns my head to face him. "What can I do?"

Choose me. Make a commitment. Prove you won't walk out of my life again. "I honestly don't know."

"You do know. You're just not telling me." His deep blue eyes burn into mine. "Did I hurt you?" He clears his throat. "I mean upstairs earlier—not my decade of stupidity."

"No."

"Are you angry Hudson overheard us?"

My face heats. "I'm a little embarrassed, but I'll get over it."

"Please tell me what's wrong," he whispers, feathering his knuckles over my cheek.

His tenderness reminds me of the Dean I knew in college. The kind, gentle soul who put everyone before himself. I'm sure that version of him is still in there, but there's something else too. A darker, more primal man lives inside him—one who isn't afraid to take what he wants. A man who is more than comfortable being in control. *That* man is a stranger. His dominance intrigues and entices me. The trouble is, I can't figure out if he exists outside the bedroom. *What if I don't know Dean as well as I thought I did?*

"I don't know how I'll handle a long-distance thing—if that's even something you'd want to try. I don't want to come between you and your family." I wrap my arms tighter around myself as the confessions fall from my lips in a rush. "Mostly, I'm scared of losing you all over again."

"I will do everything in my power to make sure that doesn't happen." He steps closer to me. "I want you, Camille. I've always wanted you. I can't guarantee I won't screw up, but I'm willing to put in the work. Please give us a chance." He cups my face and brushes his lips over mine, coaxing me into a tender kiss.

The old Dean would have never expressed his feelings. He kept everything wrapped up. Maybe I'm not the only one who's changed over the past decade.

Unwrapping my arms from my body, I pull him close and weave my fingers into his hair. He groans when I deepen the kiss. I pour my soul into it, gifting him what's left of my trust. Dean kisses me back harder, until I'm breathless and dizzy. My body comes alive when he grinds his hips against me. He's rock-hard. I'm beyond ready.

I yank my mouth from his. "Upstairs."

We rush to his room, barely making it behind the closed door before tugging each other's clothes off and falling into his bed. He settles on top of me and resumes our kiss, deeper this time. It's wild. Frenzied. Fueled by lust and hope. Forgiveness and promises.

He rolls his hips, dragging his cock through my body's slickness, then suddenly stills. "Fuck."

"What's wrong?"

"I don't have any more condoms."

"I'm on the pill, and I haven't been with anyone in three years. All my tests were negative." After Ryan cheated, I asked my doctor to run every available test. Twice.

"It's been over a year for me, and I've always used protection."

"I trust you."

"I trust you too." He surges forward, filling me with one thrust. "You feel so fucking good." His words come out on a groan as he starts to move.

I wrap my arms and legs around him and clutch his back, moaning when he deepens his thrusts. Our lips collide, tongues tangling as we battle for control of the kiss. He'll win eventually but fighting him makes my surrender sweeter. We lose ourselves to the rhythm of our bodies joining, moving as one. Sex with Dean is a homecoming. I'm not a performer; I'm cherished. Safe. Secure.

He slides his hand beneath me and squeezes my ass, brushing his lips over my ear. "You're mine. You know that, right?"

"Yes." My breathless reply earns me another ass squeeze.

"You're a gift, sweetheart." He kisses my neck. "You're everything I've ever wanted."

I cling to him tighter as his strokes bring me closer and closer to the edge. "Oh, God, Dean. Please don't stop." I do my best to stifle my moans, but they keep breaking free as pleading whimpers.

He groans and moves faster. "I can't get enough of you."

Orgasms are a mindset. I struggled to get there with Ryan because my mind wandered. That isn't the case with Dean. He's my sole focus. I'm attuned to every sensation, from the weight of his body on top of me, to the brush of his chest hair against my nipples. His warm breath on my neck. The clench of his thigh muscles. The friction on my clit. Inside, his cock rubs my G-spot with every stroke until I spasm around him.

"Oh, *Dean*." I drag my nails down his back as I come, wildly bucking my hips into his thrusts.

"I love hearing you say my name." He picks up his pace, driving me into the bed. "You feel so good." He groans the words and fucks me harder. "Oh, fuck, I'm gonna come."

I wrap my legs tighter around him and grip his ass. "Give me everything."

Dean slams into me with a loud moan as his body releases. I pull him deeper, desperate for all of him. His frenzied thrusts slow when he's given everything he has to give. Gasping, he collapses on top of me.

We hold one another in silence, our bodies still joined. The aftershocks of my orgasm ripple through me and I melt into the bed, blissed out and sated. This is what true connection feels like.

My eyes flutter open in the early morning light. I'm on my side, burrowed beneath the blankets. Dean is asleep behind me, molded to my backside with his arm and leg draped over me. I'm warm. Too warm.

I try to scoot away, but he pulls me closer. "Where do you think you're going?"

"You're making me hot."

"Already? I'm barely awake."

I pinch his thigh. "I mean literally hot. Plus, I need to pee."

He releases me immediately. "Be my guest, sweetheart."

I scramble from the bed and cross the room, well aware of his gaze locked on to my naked ass. I close the door behind me. A woman needs her privacy after all. I quickly do my business and wash up, then swish some toothpaste around and fix my hair. Once satisfied, I leave the bathroom.

Dean is the picture of relaxation, lying on his back with his arms crossed behind his head. I pad over to the foot of the bed, making no move to cover up. His heated gaze roams from my breasts to my pussy.

"Like what you see?" I throw his earlier words back at him.

"Fuck yeah, I do. Come here."

"What if I want you to *make* me?"

His eyes darken. "Think I won't?"

I toss my hair over my shoulder and give him a flirty look. "I dunno. You tell me, Dr. West."

"Come here." When I don't move, he rises and prowls around the bed to me. "You want to do this the hard way?"

"Sure do." I chirp the words, hoping to ignite his dominant side.

Before I even know what's happening, Dean spins me around, holds my wrists behind my back and shoves me face-down onto the bed. He lowers himself on top of me, pinning my legs together with his thighs. I turn my head to the side in time to watch him reach for the bathrobe I'd worn after last night's shower. He removes the belt and ties my wrists together.

His mouth moves over my neck and shoulders like a flame. Goosebumps bloom on my skin when he kisses beneath my ear and whispers, "You look so pretty, all tied up for me." He drags his tongue up and down my neck. "Only thing missing is a bow."

He kisses his way down my spine and tightly squeezes my ass cheeks. Reaching between my thighs, he teases my clit, then slides two fingers inside me. He pumps them in and out at a leisurely pace. "You know I can do anything I want to you right now?"

"Yes." He's right. I'm completely at his mercy, and I've never felt more exhilarated.

"What's your safe word?"

"Politician." I squirm beneath him, desperate for more than his fingers inside me.

"Good girl." He continues his relaxed pace as his thumb inches dangerously close to my ass. "Has anyone ever touched you here?"

I moan when he rubs circles on areas where *no one* has ever ventured. The untouched nerve endings come alive with sensations I never thought I'd enjoy.

But I do. More than a little.

He stills. "I asked you a question."

"Only you."

Dean resumes his tantalizing strokes until I'm pleading for more. I've never been someone who asks for what she wants in the bedroom, but *this* man knows exactly how to awaken my boldness.

"Dean, I need you."

"I'm right here, sweetheart."

"If you're not inside me in the next thirty seconds, I'm tapping out on principle."

He chuckles and withdraws his hand, then caresses my ass cheeks. "We definitely don't want *that*."

"Then you'd better get a move on."

"Point taken." He scoots backward and tugs me up onto my knees. Kneeling behind me, he lines us up and teases me with the head of his cock. "You want me to fuck you?"

Maybe he craves reassurance after so many years of pining. Or perhaps he needs my explicit consent. The reason doesn't matter. Whatever the question, my answer for him has always been yes.

I arch my back and try to meet his gaze, which is a bit of a challenge in this position. "*Yes*."

He grips my hips and fills me with one thrust. I cry out as he starts to move with brutal, pounding strokes. His intensity makes my toes curl. I will never tire of this version of him.

"So perfect," he growls, slamming into me. "So. Fucking. Beautiful." He digs his fingers into my hips and sets a frantic rhythm, driving me into the mattress.

The blankets muffle my moans, but there's no silencing the headboard slamming the wall with each thrust.

My gaze finds the clock on his nightstand. It's only seven. I know Jordana is a light sleeper, and I'd hate to wake her—or anyone else. "Someone's gonna hear."

"Don't care." His pace doesn't falter.

The orgasm takes me by surprise, ricocheting through my core. I bite the comforter to keep from wailing his name. My body spasms around him and my legs give out. He lifts me back up.

A few more thrusts and he joins me on a guttural groan. I love hearing his pleasure. In college, I fantasized about how he'd sound when he orgasmed. Reality is far sexier.

He snatches my hands and unties me. Without pulling out, he flops onto his side and tugs me into a spooning position. He molds himself to my back and I melt into his embrace, loving the safety of his arms. I've gone far too many years without being held.

His gasping breaths gust my neck when he whispers, "I love you, Camille."

Too stunned to reply, I cling to his forearm and try to breathe. I've loved him for years. I want nothing more than for him to truly feel that way, but my insecurities don't hesitate to remind me how Ryan *only* told me he loved me after sex. The post-orgasmic fog helped him suddenly express the appreciation and affection he denied me otherwise. Dean is his twin. How deep do their similarities run? What if his declaration is an endorphin-fueled ruse? God knows I can't handle more empty words and false promises. I've heard enough for a lifetime.

I squeeze my eyes shut against the tears pricking them. Pressing my quivering lips together, I fight to hold back the sob that wants to break free. This was supposed to be a lighthearted reunion with my friends—not a whirlwind romance. We're leaving the cabin this afternoon, for fuck's sake. Did I honestly think I'd secure a commitment from Dean when all we've done is fuck?

Deep in my bones I know he can't give me what I need.

I'm furious at my own foolishness. Once again, I've done a shitty job of shielding my heart.

CHAPTER TWELVE

Dean

Mood Music: "Lost" by Dermot Kennedy

I'm not sure where I went wrong, but Camille has been quiet all day. She excused herself to her room after our romp and stayed up there for hours. She finally emerged with Lena around lunchtime. Except, she picked at her sandwich and barely even looked at me.

It's early afternoon. Everyone is busy packing up their belongings and tidying the cabin. The owner requested we leave by four so they can get things ready for tomorrow's guest arrival.

My stomach is a giant knot, and I've been staring out a window at a snow-covered Christmas tree for God knows how long.

"You OK, man?" Sawyer asks, coming up beside me.

"Yeah."

He narrows his eyes on my face. "You sure?"

"Not really." I release a heavy sigh. "She's avoiding me."

"Did something happen? I mean, other than the, uh, *event* I overheard." He smirks.

"Sorry. I didn't realize how early it was." I sheepishly meet his gaze. "And no. Nothing happened. She was fine one minute, and then she completely shut down." I point to the ceiling. "She's been upstairs 'packing' for over an hour."

"Have you tried talking to her?"

"I went to her room before, but she had Lena running interference."

"What makes you say that?"

"Lena told me Camille was napping, but I heard them chatting on my way down the hall. So, yeah. She's definitely avoiding me." My chest tightens. "I think maybe she regrets what happened this weekend."

"Or maybe she's scared?" Sawyer's gaze burns into me. "Think about it, man. This was an escape from reality, and now it's almost time to leave. Maybe she's worried about your future together, assuming there is one."

"Of course there is," I snap, crossing my arms over my chest.

He rests his hand on my shoulder. "I'm not the one you need to convince." He glances over my shoulder as Jordana enters the room, carrying brown paper bags.

"OK, I packed snacks for everyone in case you get hungry on the trip home."

Sawyer accepts his with a smile. "You're a doll, Jordy. Thanks."

"You're welcome." She hands mine over. "Please let me know when you make it back to Boston."

"I will. Thank you for the care package."

Jordana wraps me in a hug. "I'm so glad you came."

I give her a squeeze. "Me too." *I think.*

Talia appears with Jude and Hudson, and we all congregate in the living room chatting until Lena and Camille finally come downstairs. My heart rate kicks up a few notches, and my palms start to sweat at the sight of her looking beautiful in a green sweater and leggings.

I start to walk toward her, but Jude is faster.

"So, Cami." He flashes her his billionaire smile. "Since you and Dean are, well, doing whatever you're doing, do you still need a date for the wedding on Friday?"

"Oh, right. I forgot about that." She gnaws her lip and glances over his shoulder at me. "Um, I'm really not sure. I guess that depends on Dean." Hope shines in her eyes.

Everyone turns to face me.

Bile rises up my throat and my stomach hits the floor, knowing I have to disappoint her. I realize if I have any hope of keeping Camille, I need to confront Ryan—and deal with my mother—and I'm more than ready to do so. However, some sweet woman's wedding is not the place for a West family showdown. While I could easily call him this week, it's a conversation we should have in person, and I know for a fact my work schedule won't allow that until after the new year.

"Sweetheart, if it were any other wedding, you *know* I'd be there." I clear my throat. "But my brother's the best man, and if—"

"I get it." She plasters on a fake smile and addresses Jude, "I really can't handle facing Ryan alone. Will you please come with me?"

"Of course. Text me the information, and we'll work everything out." He squeezes her shoulder. "Don't worry. I've got you covered. I'll keep him away from you *and* make sure we have a good time."

Bastard.

I know he's only being a supportive friend, but I clench my fists so I don't punch him. I should be the one shielding Camille from the people who've hurt her.

She stares up at his face. "Thank you. You have no idea how much I appreciate that."

Her heartfelt words tighten my chest.

Jude hugs her. "No need to thank me. That's what friends are for, sugar."

My blood is boiling, and I can feel Sawyer's blue gaze searing my skull. I'm sure he thinks I'm a coward for not staking my claim—and maybe I am—but some things take precedence over what I want. Even though I can't stand Ryan, he's still my brother. I don't want to chance a public altercation that could affect his campaign. I'm a better man than that. He and I will have the Camille conversation in private, as soon I straighten out my schedule. I hope she understands my reasons for waiting.

Although I'm starting to wonder if I still believe in my own convictions.

Lena raises her eyebrow as if begging me to reconsider. I toy with the idea for a moment, and imagine myself throwing caution to the wind, but no matter how much I'd love to tell my brother to fuck off, I can't. I refuse to be the guy who selfishly jeopardizes someone else's future. Drake Reynolds, the groom, is a bigshot lawyer with ties to the press. My unexpected appearance—as Camille's date—would undoubtedly raise eyebrows, and likely gain media attention. Ryan has dreamed of being a US senator since we were kids. As much as I hate myself for backing down, I owe it to him—and my mother—to sit this one out for now. Jude will be her moral support at the wedding, and I'll make it up to her the following weekend, when we celebrate the new year together.

Hopefully.

After gathering our belongings, we lock up and head outside. Hudson and Sawyer help Jordana and Talia carry their bags, and Jude grabs Camille's and Lena's before I even have the chance to offer. I trudge toward my SUV like an idiot, unsure how to make things right.

Everyone hugs after loading up their vehicles. The guys head out, followed by Talia and Jordana, until Lena, Camille, and I are the only ones left.

Lena opens the door of Camille's Beetle and slides into the driver's seat. "I'm excited to drive this bad boy. Nice meeting you, Dean. Get home safely."

"You too, Lena. Merry Christmas and happy early birthday."

"Thanks." She grins and starts the car. "Well, I'll let you two chat while this warms up. Take your time, Cami." She closes the door.

My heart pounds in my chest when Camille meets my gaze with desolation in her beautiful green eyes. "It was nice to see you, Dean."

I step closer to her. "Nice to see me? You say that like we didn't spend the weekend pouring our hearts out to each other. You say it like this is . . . goodbye." I can barely push the word out.

"It is, isn't it?"

"Not even close. Look, I don't know what I did, but I'm sorry," I stammer, knotting my hands in my hair.

She squeezes her eyes shut. "I'm sorry too."

"Sorry for what?" She has nothing to apologize for.

Regret shines in her eyes when they finally meet mine. "For getting carried away. The truth is, I can't do this." She motions between us. "I know I suggested it before, but I really can't handle a long-distance relationship. I need so much more than that. Besides, our history is too complicated. There are other people to think about."

"I don't give a fuck about anyone else." My voice breaks, and my chest caves in as I try to process her words. "They don't matter." The realization arrives eleven years too late, but I'll do everything in my power to fix the damage I've caused.

"But they do, though. They matter an awful lot."

Yeah, they do, but so does she. I reach out to take her hand, but she pulls it back.

She slowly shakes her head. "You forget how well I know you. You care *deeply* about how other people feel. I'm not faulting you for that—it's a wonderful trait to have—but I don't want to be the reason you're at odds with your mother. It's not fair for me to put you in a shitty position like that." She shrugs and blinks rapidly. "I like your mom. I respect her. I respect *you*, Dean." She releases a shaky breath. "And family comes first."

"But I want you." My lame protest doesn't do the cleaver cracking my chest wide open any justice. All that's left of my pathetic heart plummets to the ground, turning the pristine, white snow a deep scarlet. God knows I'd rather bleed out than feel what I'm feeling. "Camille, please. I want you."

I'm ready to fall to my knees and beg her to reconsider. Wrap myself around her legs. Tie myself to the bumper of her little blue clown car, so she can't leave.

But, like always, I do nothing.

"I want you too." A tear rolls down her cheek. "But I need more than you can give me."

A million thoughts collide in my head. I open my mouth to explain my plan, make sure she knows I'm ready to face Ryan *after* the wedding, but the finality of her words renders me mute.

The truth is, she's undeniably right. She deserves more than I have to offer. She should have a man who can take care of her. Hold her in his arms every night. Make her laugh. Dry her tears. Prepare a nice dinner for her after a long day. Support her writing endeavor. Learn and grow with her. A man who can welcome her into his family without fear of tearing it apart.

I could be that guy if she'd give me some time to figure things out, but it looks like she's already made up her mind.

My eyes burn, nostrils flaring with my attempt to keep my composure. "So, I guess that's it, then?"

"Yeah," she whispers, as tears stream down her cheeks.

"Merry Christmas," I croak, swallowing tightly.

I clench my jaw instead of telling her how much I love her, or begging her not to leave me, because she clearly doesn't want to hear those things from me. She already made her decision.

"You too. Please take care of yourself, Dean. Maybe I'll see you at our next reunion." With that, she makes her way to the passenger's side and gets into the Beetle, closing the door with a loud thud.

Rooted in place, I can't move or breathe.

Lena gives me a wave and eases the car down the driveway. My vision blurs, watching them leave. I'm not a crier, but warm tears spill over and dampen my cheeks out of spite.

Soon, the taillights disappear from view, and I'm alone.

Just like always.

CHAPTER THIRTEEN

Camille

Mood Music: "No Light, No Light" by
Florence + The Machine

Lena squeezes my hand tighter. "I know you're hurting right now, but I'm proud of you for standing your ground instead of settling."

"Thanks." Tears stream down my cheeks as I stare at the scenery whizzing past me. We've been on the road an hour, and I've already used all the napkins in my glovebox. "It's like you said, there has to be more than what goes on in the bedroom. I need a commitment, not a vague 'we'll figure it out.' I don't want to invest my time in something that will only break my heart. More than that, I want a man who's willing to fight for me."

"I can't believe he let you walk away."

"I can. He's done it before." My heart cracked down the center when Dean stood there, content to say his goodbyes like what we shared didn't matter. I know I was the one who initiated our split, but it would have been nice to feel like I was important to him. "He clearly hasn't changed much since college. His loyalty to Ryan will always take precedence—as it should, I guess—but I can't live like that. It's not healthy for me to be around Ryan's narcissism. I dealt with it for eight years."

"When Jude brought up the wedding earlier, I kept hoping Dean would stake his claim." She sighs. "I feel like he really wanted to."

"I'm sure he did, but his wants have never been his priority. He's more concerned with keeping the peace." Dean may have a big dick, but he's proven he has no backbone. I squeeze my eyes shut. "I get the loyalty aspect, but it's not like I asked him to divulge Ryan's darkest secrets on live television, you know? All I wanted was a fucking date." I glance over at her. "Someone to dance with."

Moral support for when I have to face the man who hurt me for the first time in three years.

"I'm sure you'll have fun with Jude. He seems like a good guy."

"He is."

"He's also really fucking hot, so . . ."

I give a watery laugh. "Jude *is* gorgeous, but I don't have those kinds of feelings for him."

She shimmies in her seat. "Maybe his dance moves will make you reconsider."

"Doubtful."

"In all seriousness, thank you for letting me tag along this weekend. Your friends are awesome, and I had a great time connecting with them. I can't wait to go aggravate Sawyer at the pharmacy."

"I'm glad *you* got to spend time with them."

"Why do you say it like that?"

A sigh heaves from my chest. "I dunno, I guess I'm annoyed with myself for being so hyper-focused on Dean, that I practically ignored everyone else. I mean, Sully is going through a rough patch, and we never had a chance to have our heart-to-heart. I can't imagine what he's going through, trying to raise a little girl by himself."

"Yeah. That's gotta be hard."

"Seriously. I want to be there for him." I blow my nose again. "I also didn't see any of Jordy's renovation pictures *or* talk to Talia about her experience with having pharmacy students at her store for the first time. Not to mention, Hudson is clearly dealing with some shit with the sleepwalking. I feel like an asshole for neglecting my friends because I was too busy having sex."

"You're saying you regret sleeping with Dean?"

"Yes and no." A fresh wave of tears fills my eyes. "It was *by far* the best of my life, but now I know what I'm missing."

I would have been better off not having a taste of what could have been. Those blissful twenty-four hours were nothing more than a cruel tease. I'm back to where I started, except now I have the pain of knowing how perfect we could be together.

If only he'd chosen me.

"Do you love him?"

"I've always loved him, Lena." A tear escapes. Then another. "But sometimes love isn't enough."

Rupert is curled up in my lap, purring softly. Despite what he thinks, the enormous Maine Coon is really too big to be a lap cat. I scratch between his ears. "You feel heavier, dude. Did Jen overfeed you?"

He slow blinks and nuzzles my hand.

"Yeah. I thought so." I nudge Alastair, who's snuggled by my feet, beneath the blankets like always. He's the reason just about everything I own is covered with orange fur. "And what about you?"

He chirps, stretching out his body along my shins.

I glance at Nigel, who's seated on the coffee table. He spent the afternoon staring at me while I read—no doubt judging me for lazing around all day. With his paws tucked beneath him, and his perpetual bratty expression, my black Persian is the picture of pompous regality.

"Did you miss me, Nigel?"

He yawns.

"Figured as much." Sighing, I return my attention to the book Lena dropped off when she checked on me earlier.

I desperately need an escape from my mind's torment, but I haven't had the motivation to write since returning from my upstate trip four days ago. Truthfully, I haven't had the energy to do much of anything since I called things off with Dean.

The fleeting taste of happiness destroyed me. I was better off not knowing. I could have trudged along in my boring existence beneath the comforting blanket of ignorance.

But nope. I went against my better judgment and pursued something I had no business pursuing. I danced with the devil and got burned.

And it hurts so fucking much.

After eleven years of not speaking, I should be used to missing him, but it goes much deeper this time. We connected and shared truths we'd never dared to speak of. He let me see his heart, and I showed him mine. Now the ache is unbearable. I can't stop thinking about him. His eyes. The way he held me. How good it felt to be wanted, even if it was only for a little while.

I know Lena said I shouldn't settle for less than I deserve, but now I'm second-guessing my decision to walk away. Maybe I should've held on tighter.

After all, I did exactly what I accused Dean of doing when I wrote off our relationship instead of giving it a chance. Maybe we could have *figured something out*. Now, I'll never know. I pull Rupert closer and bury my face in his fur as my eyes well with tears. Again. They roll down my cheeks in silence, and I cling to my cat, wishing for Dean's arms around me.

Stop it, Cami.

I need to get my shit together before I face Ryan tomorrow. It's bad enough I'll have to see *him* after everything he put me through. Now it'll hurt even more, given his resemblance to Dean. A sob wracks my frame, my tears dampening Rupert's fur. What a mess I've gotten myself into. Even if Ryan weren't the best man, I'd still be kicking myself for agreeing to attend a Christmas Eve wedding when I should be home, eating cookies and watching *Elf*.

Tomorrow is also Lena's birthday. I'm taking her out for breakfast to celebrate. Hopefully, she'll give me the mother of all pep talks, so I can survive this wedding.

My phone rings, startling Nigel, who scurries out of the room. I release Rupert and wipe my face, then reach for the device and glance at the screen. It's Jude. He's one of those rare people who don't believe in texting.

"Hello?" I answer with forced cheerfulness, hoping he won't be able to tell I've been crying.

"Hey, Cami. I just wanted to touch base about tomorrow."

I groan and squeeze my eyes shut. "You have no idea how badly I want to fake an illness to get out of going. No offense to you, obviously, but I'm dreading it with every fiber of my being."

His deep chuckle rumbles in my ear. "Oh, stop. We'll have fun. I won't let that asshole ruin your night."

"Pretty sure being in the same zip code as him is enough to do the trick."

"It's all about mindset, sugar. If you go into it thinking the night is gonna suck, it probably will, but I need you push those thoughts aside and trust me."

"I'll try."

"If you remember from school, Senator Dickwad never liked me. He'll definitely keep his distance when he sees us together."

"What if he doesn't though?"

"I'll handle it. Listen, all you need to do is show up in your pretty dress, smile and nod a few times, hug the bride, and take advantage of the open bar."

"Please don't let me get too shitfaced."

"How shitfaced is too shitfaced? Because you could definitely use a few drinks. I mean, are you worried about getting tipsy, or do you just want to avoid the level of drunk you were when I rescued you from that frat party?"

I shudder, thinking about how close I came to having sex with three football players from another college. It was right before Thanksgiving break. My roommates and our guy friends had gone home for the holiday. Since Jude didn't have a home to go to, and I had to work at the coffee shop all weekend, we chose to stay on campus. I wasn't dating Ryan yet, but I'd already humiliated myself trying to kiss Dean.

I was sad and lonely as fuck when I crashed a party my coworker had mentioned. I have no idea how much vodka I drank that night. I don't know who answered my ringing phone when Jude called to check on me after I didn't come home from work. That guardian angel—whomever it was—gave him the party's address. I can't fathom what would've happened if he hadn't shown up.

I vaguely remember being forcibly kissed by more than one

guy, but then I blacked out. Although a chunk of time is missing, my memory holds flashes of a scuffle.

The next morning, I woke up on Jude's couch, wearing his clean clothes, with a puke bucket beside me. He was sporting a black eye and a split lip.

He relayed how he busted into a room where a trio of guys had me partially undressed. I was barely conscious, but they were still clothed, which made him believe the worst hadn't yet happened. He said he went apeshit and dragged me out of the bedroom, then brought me back to his place. Once we were safely in his suite, he stripped me down and put me in the shower—twice—because I kept barfing all over myself. He slept on the other couch so he could keep an eye on me. Then, after breakfast, he drove me to a clinic to get checked out—just in case his earlier assumptions were incorrect.

"Slightly tipsy is OK. I don't want to be anywhere near the level of drunk I was at that party. Like, ever again. I try not to think about that night." Or talk about it. I was too ashamed to tell my roommates what happened. Jude kept his mouth shut too. To this day, he and I are the only ones who know about my stupidity.

"Same here. I'm sorry I brought it up." He clears his throat. "My point is, I need you to trust me about the wedding. I'm driving, so you're more than welcome to have a few worry-free drinks. I won't let you get wasted, and I promise to get you home in one piece."

"Thanks for having my back."

"I'll always have your back, Cami. What time do you want me to pick you up?"

"The ceremony starts at four, so three would be great. That will give us plenty of time to get there in case there's traffic."

"Perfect. I'll see you then. Do me a favor and relax, OK?"

"I'll try." I'm not sure the word *relaxation* is in my vocabulary, but I don't want to burden Jude with that.

We end the call, and I return to my book, comforted by the fact that I'll have moral support for the wedding I want to skip.

Now if only I could skip ahead to the part where my heart stops hurting.

CHAPTER FOURTEEN

Dean

Mood Music: "You're the Only Place" by Josh Groban

MY MOTHER IS THE REIGNING QUEEN OF disappointment, and she has zero qualms when it comes to making people aware of her disdain. Her current problem? Me. I was supposed to take her to Midnight Mass at her church because she loves the Christmas Eve festivities, but I had the audacity to cancel.

It's noon. I just woke up after working the overnight shift at the hospital. It was crazy in the ER—like it always is during the holiday season—and I'm too fucking tired to deal with my mother's dramatics.

"I never see you."

"We had lunch two days ago," I remind her, pinching the bridge of my nose. I'd eaten three quarters of my meal—while listening to her drone on about my brother's campaign—before she even asked how I was doing. Not that I would've told her about my broken heart, but still. It would've been nice to feel like I mattered for once.

"Ryan won't be around either. What, am I supposed to sit in a pew all by myself?"

"Ask Gail." She's my mother's ornery, judgmental neighbor. Gail likes to complain almost as much as Mom does. I'm sure they'll love criticizing the other parishioners' outfits.

"I don't want to go to church with Gail, I want to go with you." She sounds like a petulant toddler now, and it's pissing me the fuck off.

I squeeze the phone in a vise grip. "I'm sorry, but I can't take you this time."

"What could possibly be more important than spending time with your mother?"

"Gee, I dunno, my fucking mental health," I snap, as decades of frustration bubble over.

"Dean Thomas West, you watch your mouth when you speak to me."

"Watch my mouth?" I release a humorless laugh. "Funny, I expected something along the lines of, 'Are you OK?' but evidently, that's too much to ask."

"Excuse me?"

"Look, I'm sorry I can't do church tonight, but I am thirty-four years old. I don't need to explain my reasons to anyone."

"I don't care how old you are, I'm still your mother, and I don't like your tone."

"There really isn't much you *do* like about me, is there?"

"What the hell is that supposed to mean?"

Her indignance infuriates me almost as much as the truth in my words. I have never been good enough in her eyes. Nothing I accomplish will ever compare to the golden child. I am forever second best.

"You know what? It doesn't matter. Merry Christmas, Ma. I'll talk to you next week." I end the call and flop onto my bed.

I stare at the wall for a few minutes, wallowing like I've been doing since I left New York. It's Christmas Eve, and I'm alone once more. What would my life have been like if I'd demanded the attention I needed? What if I was the one who people made sacrifices for? I tasted happiness when Camille was in my arms. I saw a glimpse of what we could have shared. But I let her walk away. Now the hollow hunger aches deeper than it did before I knew how perfect we were together.

The anger inside me flares to life, burning with the heat of a wildfire. I snatch the phone and dial my mother's number.

She answers on the first ring. "I hope you're calling to apologize."

"I'm not."

"Have you changed your mind about church?"

"Nope." I clench the phone in my fist. "Would it have killed you to ask why I'm upset?"

"What are you talking about?"

"Maybe I didn't want to be the strong one all the time. Maybe I needed more from you. Weren't my needs important? Didn't *I* deserve the fucking advantage now and then?"

To my surprise, she doesn't reprimand me for swearing. "You aren't making sense."

"You were always so concerned with Ryan. Everything was about him. All I ever heard was Ryan this, Ryan that, Ryan, Ryan, Ryan. What about me? Didn't I matter to you?"

"Of course you did. What the hell kind of question is that?"

"You've always treated me like a second-class citizen."

"That's not true."

"Bullshit."

"Where is this coming from?" She has the audacity to sound confused.

"When was the last time you asked about my life?" I snarl, squeezing the phone in a death grip now.

Several moments pass before she finally speaks. "Is something going on with you?"

"There's a lot of shit going on, Ma. There always is. You've just been too busy worrying about Ryan to notice."

"Well, his campaign—"

"Fuck his campaign. What should I do to be worthy of your interest? Fly a fucking spaceship to the moon? Run for President? Get shot by a sniper?"

"Jesus Christ, Dean! You're talking crazy right now."

"You know what's crazy? I've spent my whole life waiting for something I'm never gonna get. I'm fucking hurting, and you don't even care. That's fine though. I'm used to it. Go ahead and make some more Senator West stickers to stick all over the fucking place. Don't worry about me. I'll keep doing the same shit I've been doing." I hang up and throw my phone across the room.

My head is throbbing, and I want to punch something, but I roll to my side and stare out the window instead. I'm not sure whether I feel guilty for screaming at her, or relieved to get things off my chest. All I know for sure is the aching void where my heart used to be.

My phone rings. Convinced it's my mother calling to tell me what a shitty son I am, I stagger across the room and snatch it off the floor to silence the ringer. Sawyer's name appears on the screen. I don't feel like talking, but I answer anyway.

"Hello?" Plopping onto my bed once more, I press the speaker icon, too lazy to hold my cell.

His voice fills the room. "Hey. What's up?"

"Absolutely nothing. You?"

"Same. Kerrigan is with Sandra tonight and tomorrow."

"I thought she couldn't see her until your divorce is final?"

"It's a court-mandated, *supervised* visitation at my mother-in-law's place. Unfortunately, I have no choice in the matter. I won't get Kerrigan back until tomorrow afternoon, which means I'll miss out on watching her open presents from Santa." The sadness behind his words is a punch to the stomach.

"I'm sorry, man."

"Thanks. It really sucks."

"Why can't you guys work something out for Kerrigan's sake? Like, maybe let her wake up in her own bed on Christmas morning, open presents and have breakfast with both of you there, and *then* have her leave with her mom and grandma? Or what if *you* go to your mother-in-law's place for breakfast?"

"Sandra told me to go fuck myself when I suggested that."

"Jesus."

"Yeah. Nice, right? Merry Christmas to me." He sighs, and the unmistakable sound of a beer can opening reaches my ears. "Hopefully, next year will be better."

"How is the custody stuff coming along?"

"She's fighting me tooth and nail, but given the circumstances, my lawyer thinks I'll get full custody. I have no problem with allowing supervised visitation, but I want my daughter living in a stable home, where I *know* she's safe." He hasn't told me all the details of his separation, but he hinted at something drug-related when we talked last weekend. "Anyway, what are you up to tonight?"

"I was supposed to take my mother to church, but she was being difficult, so I canceled. I don't need her drama in my headspace right now. Then we had a fight—as in, I screamed at her because she acted like I was crazy for having feelings—and I hung up on her."

"Good for you."

"You mean you *don't* think I'm a terrible excuse for a son?"

"Not at all. It's refreshing to see you express yourself and set boundaries for once. You should really do more of that." His long pause tells me he's chugging his beer. "Speaking of expressing yourself, have you reached out to Cami?"

"No."

"Why not?"

"Because she doesn't want me in her life."

"That's bullshit, and you know it."

"No, it's true." I quickly give him the rundown of my last conversation with Camille, including how I dissolved into a blubbering mess in the cabin's driveway.

"So, you just stood there and let her leave?"

"What the hell was I supposed to do? Jump on the hood of the car?"

"Dean, you're one of my best friends. I mean this with love, but you're a fucking idiot. You didn't even *try* to fight for her."

"But—"

"No buts. When something—someone—is important to you, giving up isn't an option. Even when the odds are against you. Even when you don't think you deserve the outcome you hope for, you fucking fight."

"She told me she can't do a long-distance relationship."

"So what? My lawyers told me the court often favors the mother in divorce situations. Does that mean I accept defeat and allow Kerrigan to live with a lunatic? Absolutely not. I will spend my every last dollar until I find a lawyer who can deliver. I won't stop until my baby is safe. I love my daughter, so I'm gonna fight for her. You love Camille, so why are you sitting on your ass? You should be at that wedding, dancing with your woman."

"She already has a date. She's going with Jude, remember?"

"Yeah, I remember. And if I recall, you had the opportunity to take his place. Cami wanted *you* on her arm tonight. I could see the hope in her eyes when she asked. We *all* could."

"You think I wanted to disappoint her?"

"You turned her down, didn't you?" He doesn't wait for my answer. "I've got news for you, man. Big Shot has wanted her for *years*. He kept his distance out of respect for you, but one of these days he'll make his move. Are you going to let it happen tonight?"

My blood boils with the thought of Camille in Jude's arms, but my brain's default mode kicks in. "But Ryan's gonna be at the wedd—"

"But Ryan, my dick!" Sawyer bellows into the phone. "*Enough* with the buts! Jesus Christ, Dean. Do you hear yourself? I could sit here and list out all the obstacles I'm facing. But Sandra. But the court. But having no clue how to be a single parent. But, but, but. I could wallow in misery and accept defeat. Am I doing any of that? Fuck no. I'm *fighting*. Bottom line, if you love that woman, you fight for her."

"It's more complicated than what I want, Sully." The statement leaves my lips automatically, but for some reason, it doesn't hold its usual weight. Maybe it's the anger simmering in my veins from yelling at my mother, or my frustration with myself for fucking up everything, but I'm no longer convinced my life is all that complicated.

"Only because you're making it that way. I'm tired of you always coming up with excuses for your unhappiness. Your own inaction is the reason you're miserable. You let Cami walk away from you eleven years ago, and you did it again last week. For what? Feelings of loyalty toward your asshole brother, who only cares about himself? Respect for your mom, whose head is so far up Ryan's ass, the only thing she sees is shit? Why are you giving them that power? Would they do the same for you?"

"No. They wouldn't." I make the admission without thinking, then sit bolt upright in a moment of clarity. Reeling, I drag both hands over my face as the pieces fit themselves together in my head. "They'll never be the ones who put in the work."

My idea of loyalty and respect doesn't align with what my family believes. Their actions speak for themselves. Why has it taken me this long to finally see that? Forget my mother's neglect, the whole sibling dynamic is one-sided. Ryan basks in the glory of his success, reaping the benefits at my expense, while I wallow in defeat.

He wins, I lose.

He thrives, I hurt.

All because I accepted his terms without question. I clench my fists, enraged by my history of martyrdom.

"My point, exactly. You can choose to sit ringside for the rest of your life, or you can dig out your gloves. What's it gonna be, my friend?"

I'm done with being passive. I launch myself off the bed and stalk to my dresser, snatching Ryan's most recent campaign flyer. His pompous face stares back at me, and it finally clicks.

He and Mom were never the problem to begin with. *I was*. I made myself a fucking martyr, and now I've hurt Camille even more. Eleven years ago, I stood back when she fell into Ryan's arms. I let him seduce her when she should've been mine. He would never have hurt her if I'd manned the fuck up and gone after her. But I didn't.

And now? History is repeating itself because I didn't learn my lesson. I allowed her to walk away from me last weekend when I should've held on to her. I'm the one at fault for our breakup. I've done nothing but hurt the woman I love.

I'm the true villain in this story.

The realization plows into me, and I stumble backward clutching my chest.

All my life I've stepped aside so Ryan could move forward. Accepted defeat without question. Sure, my family walked all over me, but I *allowed* myself to be their doormat. Well, guess what? I'm tired of being trampled. My days of putting myself last are over. I deserve a victory for once, and Camille deserves a hero, not a spineless fuck who can't stand up to his own family.

I tear his photo in half, crumpling it in my fist. "I want to be in the ring."

"It's about fucking time."

CHAPTER FIFTEEN

Camille

Mood Music: "It Came Upon a Midnight Clear" by Norah Jones

As far as marriage ceremonies go, this one was short, sweet, and relatively painless. Even though my stomach was twisted in a giant knot, I kept my gaze riveted on the bride, and never once made eye contact with my ex. I refused to give him the satisfaction. Jude said Ryan stared at me throughout the whole thing. Good. He should stare. I look beautiful in my red satin gown.

He wasn't the only one staring when Jude and I showed up in his expensive sports car. Whispers of, "Oh my God, that's Jude Holland!" filled my ears as we strolled into the venue. It amazes me how people flock toward the ones with money. Granted, Jude is a literal billionaire—and he looks *beyond* stunning in his suit and tie—but everyone's acting like he's royalty. When I asked if the attention bothers him, he shrugged and said, "It's all part of the job, sugar."

I can't imagine being in the spotlight like that.

We make our way to one of the smaller ballrooms at Hotel Polaris for the cocktail hour, claiming a table in the far corner.

He sips his whiskey—the one alcoholic drink he's having tonight—and surveys the room. "This place is nice."

"I know. I've always loved this venue. My job has their annual New Year's Eve bash here, so I'll be back next week. I love how it's all Christmassy," I murmur, taking in the garland and twinkling lights. "I hope they keep the decorations up until after the new year."

"Most places do."

"If not, they really should. It's gorgeous." I admire the row of decorated trees on the opposite side of the room and make a mental note to have a closer look at their ornaments. The festivity seeps into my soul, calming me and chasing away the sadness I've clung to all week. The fog is lifting, and no matter what happens tonight, I'll get through it. Even the string quartet near the bar is playing their version of "It Came Upon a Midnight Clear."

"You look beautiful, Cami."

"Thank you."

He points to my gingerbread martini. "Is it any good?"

"Delicious. Here, try some." I hold the glass out to him.

Jude sips it and smiles. "It's like a dessert."

"Right? I need to con the bartender into giving me the recipe."

"You won't need to con him. Just smile and he'll fall at your feet like the rest of the men in this room." He spots something over my shoulder and stiffens.

"What?"

He moves closer and wraps his arm around my waist, possessively gripping my hip. "Incoming."

I glance behind me, tensing when I discover Ryan is on his way across the room. He's just as gorgeous as when I last saw him, and like I expected, my thoughts jump to Dean. A wave of pain makes my heart clench. My lungs trap the air inside them.

"Just breathe, sugar," Jude murmurs.

Ryan stops at our table and sweeps his gaze over me. "It's been a while, Cam."

"It has."

"You look great."

"Thanks." I sip my martini, hoping the alcohol kicks in soon.

His eyes dart to Jude and narrow. "Holland, I didn't know you'd be here."

Jude flashes his billionaire smile. "I'm a man of opportunity, *Senator*." His patronizing tone makes Ryan scowl. Then he ups the ante by kissing the top of my head and pulling me closer. "I'd be a fool to turn down a date with a beautiful woman."

Ryan searches my face with the same assessing look he'd use when we were a couple. "Are you two together now?"

"Her love life is none of your business."

"I wasn't asking you," he snaps, clearly annoyed by Jude's smug retort. His eyes find mine once more. "So? Are you?"

"Why does it matter?" I prop my hands on my hips. "Are you still seeing Tiffany?" My lip curls on the name of the woman he cheated on me with.

"No. We split up last year. She, uh, didn't have my best interest at heart." The bastard has the balls to look sheepish.

"No kidding."

Ryan's eyes burn into mine. "Can we talk in private?"

Jude tightens his hold on me but doesn't speak up.

"I'd rather not." I slide one of my hands down to cover Jude's, interlacing our fingers. He gives me a reassuring squeeze. "As you can see, I have a date."

"Eight years together and you can't have a conversation with me?"

"I don't care if we were together a quarter century. I don't owe you a fucking thing."

Ryan blinks through his shock. "Well, all right then. Merry Christmas." He stalks to the bar.

My chest deflates on a giant exhale.

"You were great." Jude holds up his tumbler.

I clink my glass to his. "Thanks for literally keeping me on my feet."

"Anytime. Hopefully, he got the hint and won't bother you again." He finishes his whiskey. "How's the writing coming along?"

"It's not." I examine my fingernails for a moment before meeting his concerned gaze. "I haven't written since last weekend."

"How come?"

"My heart hasn't been in it."

"Because of Dean?" There's no judgement in his eyes, only concern.

"Mostly."

"What happened with you two? If you don't mind me asking, that is." When I hesitate, he touches my arm. "If it's too upsetting, you can tell me to fuck off."

"No, no. It's fine. I'm trying to figure out the best way to explain it." I take a steadying breath. "You probably didn't know this, but I was interested in Dean *long* before I started dating Ryan."

He chuckles. "Oh, I knew. Your chemistry was pretty obvious to anyone who spent time around you guys."

"I didn't realize that." Heat crawls up my neck and cheeks.

"Obvious or not, when I finally got the courage to make my move, he turned me down."

"I always wondered why you two suddenly stopped talking."

"I humiliated myself, which is why I got so drunk at the party we don't speak of. Then, if that fiasco wasn't enough, my wounded pride made me think it wise to date his twin instead."

"Yeah, not gonna lie, *that* was kinda shocking."

"I know. I wasn't thinking clearly. I mean, I *did* develop feelings for Ryan, but they were nothing compared to what I felt for Dean. Ryan was a shitty substitute. I can't believe I stayed with him for eight years."

"Don't beat yourself up." He pats my shoulder. "We all do dumb shit sometimes."

"True story. Anyway, I didn't expect to see Dean at the cabin, and I definitely wasn't prepared to fall for him all over again. I let down my guard, and things moved too fast."

"You're not college kids anymore. Who says it was too fast?"

"Jude, we went from eleven years of not speaking, to sex in twenty-four hours. Now we're back to not speaking." I squeeze my eyes shut and force myself to breathe through the wave of sadness flooding me. "Logistically speaking, we're a bad idea. I mean, he lives in Boston, for God's sake. I can't handle a long-distance thing. Not to mention Ryan and all the drama that comes with him."

"You make a valid point."

"It isn't fair for me to come between Dean and his family—not that he'd choose me over them in the first place, but that's another story. Either way, it wouldn't be right. Bottom line, he can't give me the commitment I need. He's not the kind of man who'd fight for me."

Jude rubs his jaw. "You seem so sure about that."

"Well, it's true. He didn't even try to stop me from leaving.

Some pathetic part of me hoped he'd realize I'm worth holding on to."

"I think he knows your worth, Cami."

Tears prick the backs of my eyes. "Knowing and doing are two different things."

The reception ballroom is even more gorgeous than where they held the cocktail hour, filled with enough decorated Christmas trees and twinkling lights to put the North Pole to shame.

"This place is like an enchanted forest," Jude marvels, guiding me to our table. "It's impossible to not feel the Christmas spirit."

"I know, right?" I release a blissful sigh and take in my surroundings. "Oh my God, look!" I point to the centerpiece, a breathtaking miniature village, complete with lights and a working train.

A boyish grin transforms his handsome face. "I had a train like that at one of my foster homes." He glances at me. "Well, it wasn't *mine*, but my foster dad let me play with it."

"That's sweet," I murmur, envisioning him as a little kid. "My grandmother had a similar village. She let me help set it up every year."

"I wish I had grandparents. It would've been nice to make those kinds of memories," he says sadly. I give his arm a sympathetic squeeze as he pulls out a chair for me. "Milady."

"Thank you." I settle and place my napkin on my lap, hoping the guests at our table won't be as annoying as the people who crowded Jude earlier. Several women had the nerve to ask for selfies with him. Naturally, he was as gracious and kind as he's been since the day we met. I was more than a little frustrated on his behalf. The man has been through so much; it would be nice if he could attend an event in peace.

He sits in the chair next to mine and drapes his arm over my shoulders. "I'm hungry."

"Me too." I was too anxious about Ryan to pick at any hors d'oeuvres, but now I'm starving. "The food smells amazing. I can't wait to stuff my face."

"Same. What entrée did you pick for me?"

"Filet mignon and lobster tails."

He rubs his stomach. "I apologize in advance for eating like a wolverine."

"I'll be right there with you. I'm getting the same thing."

His eyes light up. "I love lobster. The first time I ever tried it was when I treated myself to a fancy dinner after passing the boards."

I smile, thinking back to my own celebration. "I bet it tasted even better, knowing all the pharmacy school tests were finally behind you."

"Sure did." He sets his phone on the table. "I don't mean to be rude by having this out during our meal, but I'm expecting a call from one of my investors."

"No worries." I touch his arm. "I appreciate you being here in the first place. Please don't ignore your work obligations—they're *way* more important than this wedding." The device dings as if on command, and the screen lights up with a notification from something called River Myst. The circular logo features the silhouette of a mermaid. "Ooh, I *love* mermaids."

"Shit." He swipes the message off the screen. "Thought I silenced that app."

"What's River Myst?"

"Nothing." His face and ears turn pink. Snatching his water, he chugs it like that will erase the fact that I saw whatever it is that's making him blush. He shifts in his seat and sets down the nearly empty glass.

"Doesn't seem like nothing," I say wryly. Jude isn't a squirmer. Now I'm even more curious. "Just tell me."

"I can't. I signed a nondisclosure agreement."

"That sounds kinda hot. Is it a porn site or something?"

His cheeks get even redder. "I really can't tell you, Cami."

"I'm sorry, I didn't mean to be so nosy." I feel like an idiot for prying. "It's none of my business."

"You're fine," he says, as if sensing my regret. Then, after a few beats of silence, he releases a heavy sigh and leans forward in his seat. "Since I know some of your secrets, I guess I'll tell you mine." He drops his voice to a whisper. "River Myst is the cyber network affiliated with The River, a water-themed sex club where I'm a member."

"Holy shit. Those places really exist?"

A low chuckle rumbles in his chest. "Oh, I can assure you, they most certainly do."

"Wow. I'm intrigued." I never knew Jude was into kink, but now that I think about it, the idea makes sense. He's always been a thrill-seeker. "So, like, when you say *cyber*, I'm assuming you mean cam girls and such?"

He smirks. "Like I said, it's top secret, so I can't give you any details."

I sip my second martini, a chocolate peppermint one this time. "So, are you a voyeur?"

His dark gaze meets mine. "Don't ask questions you don't want to hear the answer to." Something catches his attention behind me. His eyes widen into saucers as he grips my shoulder. "Holy. Fucking. Shit."

"What?" I peer up at his face, afraid to peek at whatever has him so transfixed—in case Ryan is on his way over to bother me again. "Why'd you say that?" I clutch his hand. "Tell me."

Amusement dances in Jude's cognac gaze. "Don't worry, sugar. You're about to find out."

Someone appears at my other side and pulls out a chair. "Excuse me, is this seat taken?"

My heart stops when I recognize the newcomer's voice. *Oh my God, he's here.*

Dean settles before I can think, let alone answer. I whirl to face him. No joke, the man is so gorgeous, he takes my breath away. His tie matches his eyes, and the suit he's wearing looks like it was made for him. I open and close my mouth a few times, trying to string a sentence together.

Jude grins, his arm still around my shoulders. "How's it going, West?"

"Good. Great, actually. I've never been better." He scoots his chair closer to the table. Warmth seeps into my skin where his knee brushes against my leg.

"What are you doing here?" I finally whisper.

His deep blue gaze burns into mine. "What does it look like I'm doing?" At my bewildered stare, he adds, "I'm crashing a wedding. C'mon, sweetheart." Smirking he snaps his fingers twice. "Try to keep up."

Jude chuckles and sips his water.

"But you said you usually take your mom to church on Christmas Eve," I stammer, unsure whether the sight of him makes me want to laugh, cry, or a mix of both.

"Yup. I do." He rests his elbow on the table. "But I needed to see you, so I canceled."

I needed to see you.

I'm beyond shocked he canceled plans with his mother *and*

drove almost four hours to crash a wedding—where his brother is in attendance—just so he could see me.

"But, why?"

"So I could give you this." He hands me a folded-up piece of paper. "Go ahead, it won't bite."

"What is it?" I unfold it slowly, like I'm afraid the page will, in fact, chomp on one of my fingers.

Jude repositions his arm when Dean twists my chair to make me face him. "I finished your book for you."

"You, *what*?"

"When I asked about it at the cabin, you said you hadn't figured out which direction your story was headed, right?"

"Uh-huh..."

Dean leans forward in his seat. "You hadn't figured out the ending, so I wrote one for you." He holds up his index finger. "Mind you, it's only an outline, so you'll have to forgive my lack of creative writing ability."

My gaze darts from the paper in my hand, to his face, then back again.

Jude nudges me. "This is the part where you read the page, sugar."

"Right. OK." I turn my focus to Dean's handwritten paragraphs.

After spending thirty-four years with ringside seats, Dr. Sean East finally pulls on his gloves. He's done putting himself last. Even though he doesn't deserve (I forget the heroine's name, so I'm making her Camila), he'll do whatever's necessary to prove himself worthy of her love. Sean is ready to fight for Camila (aka the only woman he's ever been in love with), no matter what opponents join him in the ring (including meddling mothers and pompous sleazebag siblings).

Sean made a grave mistake when he allowed his woman to walk away, but he won't let it happen again. If Camila allows him back into her life, he will do EVERYTHING IN HIS POWER to keep her, up to, and including, physical restraints (read: handcuffs).

Lucky for Sean, his beautiful, funny, smart, resilient, sexy, talented, kind, and loving woman is willing to give him another chance.

(Please note, he will get down on his knees and beg if necessary.)

It takes time, patience, and the occasional screwup, but Sean wins Camila back (by following through on the promises he's made), and they live happily ever after, despite his fear of moths.

Tears blur my eyes as I read Dean's words twice. He's willing to fight for us. He truly loves me.

"Please say something."

"Dean, I—" Overwhelmed by my emotions, I meet his panicked gaze and try again. "I don't know what to say."

He cups my face. "Camille, I love you. I've always loved you. Please say you'll give me another chance."

"Dean? Holy shit, man. I thought you were in Boston?" Ryan's voice pops the bubble around us.

My stomach hits the floor.

"Fuck." Dean releases my face and straightens like he was caught with his hand in the cookie jar.

My heart sinks, knowing he's about to fall back into his old patterns. So much for him going after what he wants. That lasted all of five minutes.

"I thought you were supposed to take Mom out?"

Dean meets his gaze. "Change of plans." While he's not touching me, our chairs are facing one another, and he's caged me in with his knees. There is no mistaking the intimacy of the position.

Ryan's bewildered gaze jumps between his brother and Jude, who's casually twirling a lock of my hair. "Mind telling me what the hell's going on here?"

"Don't worry about it." Dean lifts his chin, drawing his shoulders back.

"What are you doing here?"

"Like I said, don't worry about it." Dean rests his hand on my thigh, rubbing his thumb in circles. "This may come as a surprise, but my actions don't concern you."

Ryan's gaze flicks to my lap before settling on Dean's face once more, his eyes narrowing. "What are you doing with Cam?" Not getting the answer he seeks, he addresses me instead. "I thought you were here with Holland?"

"Oh, I am." I drum my fingertips on Jude's leg, beyond grateful he didn't leave when Dean showed up. I'll need him to hold me together after Dean decides I'm not worth the trouble. I inject false calm into my voice. "We established that earlier, remember?"

Jude smiles up at him, full-on threading his fingers into my hair like he's massaging my scalp. "We're starting a polygamist colony. Wanna join? We can be brother husbands."

"Grow the fuck up, Holland." Ryan redirects his scowl to Dean, gesturing between us. "Is this some kind of joke?"

Dean eyes him. "Do you see me laughing?"

Ryan's ears turn red, like they always did when he got mad. "Can I have a word with you outside?"

"Sure." Shrugging, Dean leisurely climbs to his feet and follows Ryan out of the ballroom without so much as a backward glance.

I blink rapidly, forcing my lungs to expand on shaky breaths.

Jude settles his palm on my knee. "Hey, relax, sugar. Everything's gonna be fine."

"How do you know?"

"He's here, isn't he?"

I wrap my arms around myself in a hug. "What if he changes his mind?"

"He won't. Didn't his outline, or whatever it was, reassure you?"

"Yes, but Ryan's going to give him shit for being with me. You know how Dean gets whenever there's conflict. He'll back down like he always does." My lip quivers. "Then he'll leave again."

"May I read what he wrote?"

I hesitate for a moment, trying to decide how Dean would feel about that. Then I remember he had no problem professing his feelings in front of Jude. I hand him the letter.

His lips curve into a smile as he reads. "Moths, huh?"

"Don't you dare say a word."

He presses his hand over his heart. "I won't."

"You'd better not."

"I promise." He points to the page. "He's not going to back down, Cami. He loves you. Give him a chance to prove himself."

CHAPTER SIXTEEN

Dean

Mood Music: "Celebrate Me Home" by Josh Groban

RYAN STOMPS DOWN THE SNOWY SIDEWALK, PAUSING near the back entrance to Hotel Polaris. "What the fuck are you doing?"

"Standing out in the cold. You?"

"You know what I'm talking about." His nostrils flare when I don't respond. "Why were you sitting so close to Cam?"

"Like I told you inside, don't worry about it."

He narrows his eyes into slits. "You can't possibly be seeing her."

I clench my fists at the derision in his tone. "And what if I am?"

"We're brothers. That's crossing a line."

"Guess you can call me a line-crosser, then." I advance on him, backing him toward the building's brick exterior. "Either get used to the idea or get the fuck over it."

"She was *my* girlfriend."

I grab him by the collar. "You lost the privilege to call her your *anything* three years ago when you cheated on her." I get right up in his face, so close, our noses touch. "You're a bastard. You *knew* I wanted her, but you went after her anyway." He opens his mouth to protest, but I tighten my grip on his collar to silence him. "Don't even try to pretend it didn't go down like that. You knew exactly what you were doing when you invited her to that concert after I told you how I freaked out when she tried to kiss me. You *knew* I was trying to work up the courage to apologize and go after her."

"That's not the conversation I remember."

"You only pay attention when it's convenient for you. It's just like when we were kids. I wanted something for myself, so you made it your mission to take it from me. And for what? To belittle her writing dream? To hurt her by having multiple affairs with the gold-diggers who worked for you? To ruin her chances of getting her dream job? To crush her fucking spirit?"

He doesn't have an answer for that, but the fucker has the balls to look sheepish.

I release him and step back. "Even when she was yours, deep down, you knew she was mine. That's why you held on to her for so long. If *I* didn't have feelings for her, you would've cheated sooner."

"That's not true."

"Bullshit." I jab my finger into his chest. "You didn't deserve her, Ryan."

"And you think you do?" He sneers.

"You're goddamn right, I do." And for the first time in my life, I believe it. I'll do whatever it takes to be worthy of her love. "So, let me make myself perfectly clear. Camille is mine now, and I don't care if you, Mom, or anyone else has a problem with it. I'm not letting her go this time." Turning, I stalk to the hotel's front entrance.

He shouts something, but I'm not interested. The golden child can make all the noise he wants.

Upbeat music reaches my ears as I make my way toward the main ballroom. Camille is pacing the hallway with her arms wrapped around herself. Jude is with her, leaning against a nearby wall, listening intently to whatever she's saying. They don't see me yet, which is fine. It will give me a chance to pull myself together. I silently move closer, keeping to the shadows.

"I know you're scared, but you need to look at the facts. He's here. He ditched his mom and traveled from Boston to see *you*. And he knew damn well Ryan was going to be here *before* he came, so it's not like there was an element of surprise. He's out there having a conversation with his brother, instead of avoiding the situation. Dean is doing everything right for once."

My appreciation for Jude grows, hearing him come to my defense.

"I know, but Ryan's a manipulator. He holds a fucking PhD in gaslighting."

"No one's arguing that one, sugar." He rubs his jaw. "I have a few other words for him, but I'll spare you my tirade. Bottom line, you need to trust Dean enough to give him a chance. If he has half a brain—he's a doctor, so there's got to be something up there—he'll do right by you."

She pauses in front of him. "But what if he doesn't?"

"Then he didn't deserve you to begin with." She opens her mouth to protest, but he holds his finger to her lips. "You're a gift, Cami. Everyone who knows you, feels that way. If Dean is stupid enough to walk away from you again, he isn't worth your time." He stares at her face for a moment. "Because I *promise* you, there are men out there who'd love nothing more than to take his place." The longing in his voice makes it abundantly clear he'd be first in line.

"Thanks, Jude. You always know the right thing to say."

"It's easy to say the right thing when you speak the truth."

"Camille."

Their heads dart in my direction.

"Dean. You're back," she blurts, her widened eyes darting between Jude and me.

Knowing I overheard him, Jude holds my gaze like he's driving home his point. That's why he's been so successful in life. He doesn't need to say a word—his silence holds a power others can only dream about. He *owns* his convictions and has no problem backing them up with actions.

But he won't need to this time.

"I've been back for few minutes." I close the distance between us and cup her jaw. Brushing my thumbs over her cheeks, I stare deep into her beautiful green eyes. "And Jude said it far better than I could."

He chuckles. "I usually do."

I glance at him. "Don't gloat."

"It's not gloating when it's a fact."

"What happened with Ryan?" Camille whispers.

"We came to an understanding."

"And that was?"

I kiss her instead of answering, pouring my soul into it.

Jude clears his throat. "So, um, yeah. I think I hear a lobster tail calling my name."

Flushing, Camille breaks the kiss. "Sorry, Jude."

"I'm not." Dipping her body old Hollywood style, I kiss her again, deeper this time.

"OK, now *that's* pretty hot." He claps my back. "Wanna be brother husbands?"

"Nope," I say between kisses.

"Let me know if you change your mind."

"Not a chance, Holland. Now get the fuck out of here so I can kiss my woman in peace."

"Point taken." He laughs. "Have fun, lovebirds. Cami, I'm eating your food."

"Go for it," she says on a gasp.

He gives us a wave and heads for the ballroom.

I meet her gaze and lick my lips. "He can eat your food. I'm having something *else*."

Three sets of eyes watch my every move with varying degrees of interest. Camille's cats clearly aren't used to seeing men in her home, a fact which more than pleases me. There's an orange one peering out from beneath the couch, a black Persian guarding the kitchen doorway, and a huge Maine Coon weaving between my legs.

I lean down to scratch its head. "This one's friendly."

"Rupert is a sweetheart. He'll probably wind up on your lap at some point. Good luck. He's a meatball." Camille points to the couch. "As you can see, Alastair is kinda shy. He'll come around eventually. He likes to burrow under the covers." She juts her chin toward the Persian. "And Nigel, well, he's unpredictable."

"He's scowling at me."

"That's his normal face. He always looks like he's disgusted with the world." She hangs her coat on a hook by the door, then does the same with mine. "Don't expect much warmth from him. I'm the only one he likes."

"I'll keep that in mind."

We opted to head back to her place instead of getting a room at Hotel Polaris. This way, we can relax in bed together on Christmas morning, without having to worry about checkout times. I'm going to make French toast for breakfast and spend the whole day making love to her. Excitement courses through my body. I'm not sure how I managed to avoid getting a speeding ticket on our way here.

"Let me fill their dishes, and then I'm all yours." She rushes into the kitchen. The crinkle of a food bag sends all three cats scurrying after her.

I wait in the living room, admiring her Christmas tree. Ninety percent of the ornaments are cat themed, of course. Smiling, I brush my fingertips over a hand painted tuxedo cat family. The largest one has "Mom" across its belly, and the kittens each bear one of the cat's names.

Visions of Camille as a mother flood my mind. She would be nurturing, that's for sure. Unlike my mom, she wouldn't pick favorites. She'd love each child equally and make sure they knew their worth. She'd celebrate everyone's uniqueness and embrace the quirks that set them apart. No one would ever have to wonder if they mattered. Or whether or not they were special.

I've never given much thought to fatherhood, but I'd love nothing more than to start a family with Camille.

She approaches from behind. "In case you haven't noticed, I'm a bit of a cat lady."

I meet her gaze. "I think it's cute."

"Your brother hated it. He'd never let me have a cat because he was allergic. That's why I got three of them once we split."

"He's only allergic to bees. We had cats growing up, and he never had an issue."

"Oh, I know. He just wanted my full attention."

"Sounds like Ryan." I tilt her chin to face me. "I want your attention too, Camille. The difference is, even if you want to feed an entire colony of feral cats and become an international kitten ambassador, I'll support you every step of the way. You will always have *my* full attention." I brush my thumb over her lower lip. "I will never stop believing in you. I'll always encourage your endeavors—yes, even the nutty ones—because it makes me happy to see you excited about something."

"Thank you," she whispers, peering up into my eyes. "I love you."

"I love you too, sweetheart." I kiss her lips softly. "I will *never* stop loving you." I guide her over to the couch and motion for her to sit. Settling beside her, I take both of her hands in mine. "This is long overdue, but there's something I need you to hear."

"What's up?"

"I've been doing a lot of thinking since last Sunday, and I've learned a few harsh truths about myself. Things I'm not proud of."

"Like what?"

"Well, for starters, I've realized I need help dealing with some shit from my childhood. I don't want to make excuses for my shitty behavior, but my history of bending to my family's demands started at birth. I've never *not* put myself last, and I really don't know how to change that. There's a lot I need to work through." I brush my thumbs over her knuckles. "I want you to know I'm going to put in the effort to figure myself out, and I'm prepared to find a professional who can help me navigate it all."

Camille listens intently, her brilliant green gaze pinned to mine as she waits for me to continue.

I draw a steadying breath. "I allowed my history to dictate my actions, and in doing so, I hurt you. Not only did my initial rejection cause you pain, but my inaction when Ryan swooped in to steal you away made matters even worse. I gave you the impression you didn't matter to me when that couldn't have been further from the truth. I *know* I should have fought for you, and I'll spend the rest of my life regretting my stupidity. My cowardice. I could have spared both of us years of unhappiness." My eyes mist over. "Most of all, I'm sorry I allowed him to hurt you."

She squeezes my hands. "His actions are on him, Dean. You didn't tell him to cheat."

"No, but it wouldn't have happened if I had the balls to go after you first." I blink back the tear that wants to escape.

"I understand what you're saying, and I appreciate the sentiment, but you aren't responsible for what he did. Ryan is the one who betrayed me. I have never blamed you for the pain he caused. You also shouldn't hold yourself accountable for my actions."

"What do you mean?"

"I could have resisted his advances, but I allowed my hurt and embarrassment to cloud my judgment." She peers up at me. "I'm equally at fault."

"We'll have to agree to disagree, sweetheart." I lift her hands to my lips. "Please forgive me for the pain I've caused you." I kiss her knuckles, then press her hands to my chest, holding them over my heart. "I love you, Camille. I promise I'm going to work on myself, so I can be the kind of man you deserve. I can't guarantee perfection, but I'll figure out how to make lasting changes. I'm willing to fight for you—for us—with everything I am. Please give me a chance."

Tears shine in her eyes. "I don't want perfection, I want *you*."

"Does that mean you accept my apology?"

"Yes." She moves our joined hands over her heart. "I promise to stand by your side while you figure things out. I will love and support you, even when shit gets hard." She flashes a sexy smile. "*Especially* when it gets *hard*."

"Who's the pervert now?" I laugh and hug her, kissing the top of her head.

"I'm OK with a little perversion." She grabs both sides of my face and pulls my lips to hers.

I close my eyes as Camille deepens the kiss, threading her hands into my hair. Groaning, I kiss her like we might die tomorrow, pouring every part of my soul into it. She straddles my lap. My cock hardens between us, and I roll my hips, making sure she knows how badly I want her. How deeply I've always craved her. She's the only woman I've ever wanted for myself, and God help me, it's my turn to be selfish.

I drag my lips from hers and launch to my feet, lifting her with me. "Bedroom. Now."

She points down the hall. "That way."

We kiss and tear at each other's clothes as I carry her to her bedroom and close the door behind us. She continues stripping when I set her down, until she's in nothing but her bra and panties. I'm still wearing my shirt and pants. My tie hangs loose around my neck. Snatching the length of silk, she flashes a sultry smile and turns the lock.

"Expecting company?"

"No. Just trying to keep you here."

"I'm not going anywhere, sweetheart."

Her gorgeous eyes meet mine. "Promise?"

I take her hand and press it over my racing heart. "I'm yours even after it stops beating."

Kissing me, she places my free hand on her chest and interlaces our fingers, mimicking her actions from the living room. "Right back at you, Doc."

"Now that we've established that, I'm gonna fuck you."

"Nope." She pokes her finger into my sternum, then unbuttons my shirt the rest of the way. "I'm in charge this time. Your job is to keep quiet and do as you're told."

She tugs the shirt off my shoulders, sliding her grip down

my arms as she removes it. Next comes my belt, which hits the floor with a clunk. She pops the button on my pants and unzips them. I take over and shove them off, then kick them aside, all too eager to get naked.

She rubs my cock through my boxer briefs. "Remember the first time we got together?"

As if I could forget.

"Yeah," I grunt, breathing heavily.

"Let's do a reenactment." She holds up my tie.

I reach for it, but she yanks it away and holds it behind her back. I frown and tilt my head to the side. "But you said—"

"This time we're gonna do a role reversal. Think you can handle that?"

I'll play any role she wants, as long as I get to be inside her.

"Fuck yes."

"Pick a safe word, Dr. West."

The hunger burning in her eyes tightens my balls. As much as I love being in charge, seeing this side of her makes me crave submitting.

"Uh, let's see . . ." I rub my jaw, pondering my options. "How about moth?"

"Perfect." Camille grins and points to the bed. "Now get your fine ass over there."

I waste no time launching myself across the room like a lust torpedo, faceplanting on the mattress with the elegance of an oversized walrus.

She laughs and moves to the foot of the bed. "If you break my bedframe, we're gonna have an issue."

"I'll buy you a new one."

"Damn right, you will." She kneels on the edge of the mattress. "Roll onto your back and rest your head on my pillows. Then give me your wrists."

"Yes, ma'am." I scramble into position, waiting like a dog who knows he's about to get a belly rub. Or, in my case, a blow job.

Hopefully.

Camille reaches behind her to unhook her bra. A moment later, my mouth waters when her lush tits spill out.

"You ready?" She drops the garment onto the floor.

"You have no idea."

I think she's about to remove her panties, but she crawls up the bed to me. "Grab the headboard."

I wrap my hands around the ornate wooden spindles. Using my tie, Camille secures my wrists and leans down to kiss me. My cock jerks when her tongue slides against mine. Groaning, I fight to intensify the kiss, but she keeps her movements slow and sensual.

"Stop trying to rush me," she whispers, kissing along my jawline. She brushes her lips over my ear. "It won't work."

"Was worth a try."

She lightly nibbles my earlobe. "I'm gonna make you beg for it."

"Please fuck me." I turn my head to meet her gaze. "We're already there. This is me begging. You have no idea how badly I want you." My voice is hoarse with desperation.

Camille moves to straddle me and rolls her hips, grinding against my cock. "I want you too, but I'm going to take my time." She kisses my neck, swirling her tongue over my throat.

Every lick, kiss, and nibble drives me more insane. The anticipation of her next move heightens my desire, making me want to throw myself at her feet. I've never felt need like this.

She works her way across my collarbone, then moves lower, nuzzling into my chest hair. My hips jerk when her wet little mouth surrounds one of my nipples.

"Oh, fuck, Camille. You're killing me."

She flutters her tongue and sucks, grazing her teeth over it before moving on to the other side. Gasps and groans escape me when her soft lips travel over my abs. I tighten my stomach muscles to brace myself for what's coming next.

I need those pretty lips wrapped around my dick more than I need my next breath.

Then, as if reading my thoughts, she peers up at me with the devil in her eyes. "What do you want from me, Dean?"

"I want you to swallow my cock."

She purses her lips and tilts her head to the side like she's considering my request. "What if I were the one tied to the bed right now?" Her voice is low and husky, but it's her smile that unravels me. "What would you be doing to me?"

"I'd have my tongue inside you."

"Do you like putting your mouth on me?"

"No, I fucking love it."

"I love it too." She rises and climbs up my body until her knees are above my shoulders and her pussy is mere inches from my mouth.

I breathe in deeply, inhaling her scent, and I swear I can almost fucking taste her.

"Do you want this?" She flexes her hips, and the damp red satin of her panties tickles my nose. I wish she'd removed them first, but I'll make it work, even if I have to gnaw them off her.

"Yeah. More than you know." Lifting my head, I brush my lips over every place I can reach, my hot breath making her gasp. "Does that feel good?"

"Yes." She rolls her hips harder, moaning when she finds the friction she seeks.

"That's it, sweetheart. Take what you need." Her pussy is so close, yet too far for me to plunge my tongue inside. Her scent, and the way her soft thighs hug my face, is driving me fucking insane. I struggle against the tie binding my wrists and suck her clit through the fabric, desperate for more of this sweet torture.

Camille moans louder and grinds into me, rubbing her pussy from my chin to my nose. She's so wet, I can taste her through the material now. I release a low growl and catch the satin between my teeth.

Gasping, she stills her hips when I give the panties a forceful tug. "What are you doing?"

"Get these the fuck out of my way."

She releases a throaty laugh and moves off me for a moment, tugging the drenched satin off. Tossing the panties aside, she repositions her wet pussy above my mouth. "Better?"

I lick her up and down instead of answering, groaning at how good she tastes. This woman is my fucking ambrosia. Blind with lust, I eat her like I'll die tomorrow and she's my last meal.

"Dean," she whimpers, melting into my tongue.

"Hold on to the headboard and ride my fucking face."

Camille obeys my command like she was born to please me. My lips and tongue glide through her body's wetness with every roll of her hips. Her moans grow louder and more wanton as she chases her release.

I suck on her clit, flicking my tongue back and forth.

"Your tongue feels so good. Please don't stop." Her movements become jerkier until she lets loose a wailing moan. Her pussy pulses against my mouth but I don't stop licking until she moves off me. Gasping, she peers down at my face in shock. "Holy fuck. I never thought I'd actually enjoy doing that."

"Get used to it, sweetheart. I'm gonna make my face your new favorite seat."

"We'll see about that." She moves toward my hips and hooks her fingers in my waistband, pulling off my boxer briefs. Settling between my thighs, she grips my cock. "Your turn," she whispers, brushing her lips over the head. "Be a good boy and watch me."

My breath hisses out of me when she takes me to the back of her throat. Cupping my balls, she starts to move. Her tongue rubs the underside of my dick, and she hollows out her cheeks, showing my body no mercy.

Camille holds my gaze, even when her eyes water from my upward thrusts. I can't help myself. Her tongue feels so incredible, I'm not above fucking her mouth the way I'd fuck her pussy.

She brings me to the edge, and right before I'm about to blow, she stops. Lifting her head, she flashes a devious smile and kisses my hip bones.

"What are you doing?" I sputter, gasping and digging my heels into the mattress.

"Kissing you." She moves lower to nibble my kneecaps, then drags her tongue up my inner thighs. Massaging my balls in her hand, she licks everywhere but my cock.

I clench my jaw. "Camille, *please*."

"Please, what?"

"Suck me."

She takes the head of my cock between her lips and swirls her tongue in circles, making my eyes cross. I groan and flex upward, but she doesn't take more than the tip inside. Again, she sucks until I'm seconds from coming, then abruptly pulls back.

"You're fucking killing me."

This time she focuses her attention on my nipples, licking and kissing until my dick throbs. Then, she stops that too and feathers her fingertips up and down my sides.

"Your muscles are so sexy."

"Thanks. Please put your mouth on me."

She leans forward so her nipples brush my chest. "I love

how your chest hair feels when I rub up against you. Please don't ever shave it."

"I won't." I'll agree to anything right now, as long as she lets me come. "Now suck my dick."

Smiling, she moves between my thighs once more and tightly grips my cock. Just when I think she's about to deep-throat me, she presses a series of butterfly kisses up and down my shaft.

"Camille." I growl, thrusting my hips toward her mouth.

She takes me between her lips again and bobs her head twice before stopping. More butterfly kisses. My balls are tingling, and my dick aches with the urge to come, but she won't let me get there.

"*Please.*"

"I love how blue your eyes look when you beg." She takes me to the back of her throat, but keeps still, with just the tip of her tongue moving.

It's too much, yet not enough. I jack my hips upward, trying to get my release, but she seems determined to torture me. I can't handle any more of her edging.

"*Moth.*"

Camille releases my dick with a loud pop. "Took you long enough."

"Woman, you're lucky I'm tied up right now."

"Oh, yeah? And why's that?" She smiles sweetly and straddles my hips, lining up our bodies.

"Because you'd be facedown across my lap."

She slides down onto my dick, moaning when I fill her. Clamping her hands on my shoulders, she starts to move, rolling her hips into my upward thrusts.

We fall into a steady, fluid rhythm. Her pussy grips me tightly, coating me with the same sweet juices I can still taste on my lips. Groaning, I let my head fall back as my eyes drift closed.

"Look at me, Dean." Her gorgeous green eyes soften when I meet her gaze. "I love you."

"I love you too, sweetheart, but I can't hold out much longer."

"Don't worry, I'm already close." She picks up her pace, bouncing on my cock now. Her nails dig into my shoulders, and she arches her back. "So close."

I groan and clench my jaw. "*Camille.*"

Finally, she wails my name as her body spasms around me. I follow her over the edge approximately two milliseconds later, groaning and grunting as my cock jerks and spurts my release inside her. Camille's movements carry me through wave after wave of toe-curling ecstasy, until I slump against the mattress, completely spent.

She unties my wrists without moving off me. Once freed, I wrap my arms around her and pull her close, so her body is draped over me like a warm, soft blanket.

We hold one another in silence until our breathing and heart rates even out. I've never felt more at home than I do in her arms. Camille is the gift I've only begun to unwrap, and I can't wait to spend the rest of my life discovering her.

"Thank you for coming after me tonight," she murmurs, nuzzling even closer. "And for finishing my story."

"I meant every word I wrote. I will prove I'm worthy of you, Camille. I can't promise everything will always be easy, but I'm willing to put in the work." I kiss her forehead. "I won't let you slip through my fingers, and I swear I'll never walk away from you again."

"Good." She lifts her head to peer into my eyes. "Because I'm sure as fuck not letting you go." She kisses me slowly, tenderly moving her mouth with mine. "I really love the ending, but we'll need to iron out some plot details."

"Such as?"

"Well, for starters, what does Dr. Sean East's happily ever after look like?"

I kiss her again, deeper this time. "I don't know about him, but I'll tell you how I envision *mine*."

"Please do. I care way more about Dr. Dean West anyway."

"Good to know," I say with a chuckle. "My happily ever after is with you."

She sits up, poking my chest with her index finger. "Oh, c'mon, I need more details than *that*."

I release what remains of my doubts and fears with my breath. "With you as my wife."

Hope flares in her eyes. "Are you . . . proposing to me?"

Am I?

I hesitate for a moment, knowing it's too soon—and I don't have a ring—but does that really matter when there are concrete facts?

I know she makes my heart beat faster every time I look at her.

I know the way my soul aches when she isn't part of my life.

I know she makes me want to be a better man.

What more do I need to know? Why should society's norms keep us from going after what we truly want? Isn't our timeline the only one that matters? We wasted so many years being apart. I don't want to lose another second.

Her gaze darts away from mine, and she wraps her arms around herself. "It's OK. I was only kidd—"

"Yes." I clear my throat and abruptly sit up, then scramble into a kneeling position. "I think I am."

Camille's eyes meet mine once more and widen. Her shoulders rise and fall faster with each breath as she waits for me to continue.

"Look, I don't have a diamond to give you right now—or a fancy speech prepared—but I know I want to keep you forever." I swallow and take a steadying breath. "I realize it's kinda soon, and we have a lot to figure out, but I've loved you since we first met." I take one of her hands in mine and brush my thumb over her knuckles. "I plan on loving you until the day I die, and for the rest of eternity after that, so why wait?"

I snatch my tie and loop it over our joined hands, creating a sloppy makeshift bow, then stare deep into her eyes. "Camille Elizabeth Monet, you are a gift. I love you more than I can put into words. I want to be your husband, and the father of your children. I want us to spend the rest of our lives creating the happily ever after that works for us." I force myself to stop rambling. "I guess what I'm trying to say is, will you marry me?"

"Yes!" She yanks herself free from my bow and launches herself at me, throwing her arms around my neck. "Yes, a thousand times over."

I fall backward, pulling her along so she lands on top of me again. Our lips collide in a frenzied kiss that reaches into my soul. The victory I've waited my whole life for is finally mine.

After a few minutes, Camille breaks the kiss and stares into my eyes. "Who said you don't have creative writing abilities, Dr. West?"

"Just some people who don't matter."

"Sounds like they need a checkup from the neck up."

I laugh and pull her close, seizing her lips in another soul deep kiss. "And you, my feisty fiancée, are about to get a checkup of your own." I roll her onto her back and settle between her legs, holding her gaze when I sink inside her again.

"I love you, Dean." She kisses my lips. "But you have it all wrong."

"How so?"

"You're the gift." Camille wraps her arms and legs around me, holding on to me for dear life while I slowly make love to her.

Somehow it feels even better this time, knowing she's mine to keep.

EPILOGUE

Camille

Mood Music: "The Bones" by Maren Morris and Hozier

New Year's Eve has never been my favorite holiday because I always find it melancholic. I never make resolutions because I know I won't keep them—they're simply another opportunity for me to fail. This year, on the other hand, I'm filled with hope instead of dread.

For starters, I finally have a date for the hospital's annual party. Dean is currently at the bar, getting me a glass of champagne. Thanks to traffic delays during his trip from Boston, we arrived at the party an hour late. He apologized profusely, but I wasn't upset. All that matters is he made the effort to be here.

After spending Christmas Day together, Dean reluctantly trekked back to Boston with the promise we'd speak every day. He made good on his vow, calling whenever he could, and texting me in between. Even yesterday morning, when he was exhausted from his overnight shift, he still called to chat while I got ready for work. I won't lie, it's not easy being away from him, but I need to trust we'll figure it out.

After all, we are engaged.

The thought warms me, filling my belly with butterflies. I still can't believe it. His impromptu proposal couldn't have been more perfect, even without a ring. I nearly melted when he tied our hands together as a symbol of our bond. We haven't shared the news with anyone other than our families. We want time to enjoy our engagement before everyone starts bugging us for wedding details. Dean told his mother this morning, which is part of why he was late. He said she was confused at first—just like my parents—but once he explained his feelings, she seemed genuinely happy. Not that I'm surprised. She always liked me.

Dean approaches with two flutes of champagne, setting them on the cocktail table we claimed. "Here you go, sweetheart. The bartender said it's a fancy French one." He chuckles. "Of course, I forgot the name on my way over here, but whatever. I think you'll like it."

"I'm sure I will. French, huh?" I flutter my lashes at him. "I enjoy French things. Especially when it involves your lips."

His eyes darken as he sweeps them over me. He points to the ceiling. "We can head up to our room right now if you want."

"Not yet. I want to mingle with my friends for a bit."

Like I hoped, Hotel Polaris is still decorated for Christmas, but instead of a swanky wedding setup, the ballroom is filled with lights and music. The dance floor is full, and all around me, people are laughing and celebrating. I scan the room in search of Lena. We haven't talked since her birthday last Friday because she was out sick this week. I left messages checking in on her, but she never returned my calls. Hopefully, she's OK. Now that I think about it, she probably won't be here tonight.

"See anyone from the pharmacy?" Dean sips his champagne.

I gesture to the table of middle-aged men across the way. "Those guys are all pharmacists."

"They look . . . exciting."

I snort. "They're about as thrilling as a calculus exam."

He laughs. "So, I'm guessing you don't want to sit with them?"

"Absolutely not."

"Hey, isn't that Lena over there in the corner?" He points.

I spot her seated at a table with a gorgeous dark-haired man I've never seen before. "Yeah, it's her."

"C'mon. Let's go say hello." When I hesitate, he gives me a quizzical look. "What's wrong?"

"I don't know who that guy is, but he's definitely *not* her fiancé."

"Whoa. OK." He grimaces. "Then why is he rubbing her back?"

Sure enough, Lena's elbows are resting on the table while mystery man moves his hand in circles, massaging her upper back.

"Good question." I know Lena well enough to know she'd never cheat on Marc, but I'm more than a little perplexed by what I'm seeing. My feet carry me forward before I can stop them, and Dean follows as I make my way over to Lena's table. "Hey, you!"

She meets my gaze with reddened eyes and tearstained cheeks. "Hey, girl." Her voice lacks its usual luster. "Sorry I never called you back. It was a rough week. I've been a bit of a recluse."

"Are you feeling better? Is everything OK?"

"Not really." She glances behind me, her eyes widening in shock. "Oh, hey, Dean. Nice to see you again."

"You too, Lena."

She raises an eyebrow at me. "Uh, *clearly* we have a lot to catch up on."

"We do." My eyes dart to the mystery man who's now sipping

what looks like a seltzer. He's even more attractive up close. I hold out my hand. "Hi. I'm Camille, but everyone calls me Cami."

He smiles and clasps my hand, peering up at me with eerie gold eyes. "Nice to finally meet you, Cami. I'm Garrett." We shake.

His identity finally clicks in my mind, and I feel like an asshole for doubting my friend's character. Lena has mentioned Garrett many, many times.

"So, *you're* the infamous best friend, slash, housemate, slash, spider killer?"

He grins. "'Tis I."

Lena speaks up, "Sorry. I forgot you two haven't officially met. I swear, my brain is useless these days." She glances at Dean and motions between herself and Garrett. "I'm sure this looked *way* more scandalous than it was."

He holds up his hands in surrender. "Hey, I don't judge."

"Then you're one of the few. Anyway, this is Garrett Casey. He's been my best friend since first grade. He lives on the bottom two floors of my brownstone, and yes, he kills the spiders when I ask him to." She nudges her friend. "Gar, this is Dr. Dean West, Cami's new man."

He smiles at Dean. "Nice to meet you."

The guys shake and make small talk, quickly launching into an animated conversation about sports.

I settle beside Lena. "What's wrong?"

"Oh, you know, life and shit." She wipes her cheeks, and it's then I notice she isn't wearing her ring. "Ugh, I don't even know why I bothered trying to leave the house."

"Why'd you bring Garrett? Is Marc out of town?"

"No." She meets my gaze. "Remember when we talked at the cabin? How I told you not to settle for less than you deserve?"

"Of course."

"I finally took my own advice." She blinks rapidly to dispel a fresh batch of tears. "I called off our engagement the day after Christmas."

"Holy shit."

"Yup."

"What happened?"

"You mean besides four years of being treated like an afterthought?" She sighs heavily. "He never even acknowledged my birthday, Cami. I kept waiting, hoping he had something up his sleeve, but nope. Not even a handmade card. I mean, anyone who knows me—even the tiniest bit—is well aware I celebrate my birthday the entire month of December."

"How could you not with a Christmas Eve birthday?"

"Exactly. The man I was supposed to *marry* couldn't remember the fucking day I was born? Then he got all pissed off that my feelings were hurt. I finally had enough. I didn't want to spend my life like that, you know?"

Nodding, I give her a quick hug. "I'm really proud of you. I know it's hard right now, but you did the right thing." While I hate seeing her sad, a part of me rejoices. Marc never made her all that happy to begin with. Lena is amazing. She deserves a man who sees her worth.

"Oh, absolutely. This was a long time coming. I knew deep in my heart he wasn't the one for me. I was stupid to accept his proposal. I think I thought things would get better." She snorts. "Joke's on me, I guess."

"Are you OK?"

"Not yet, but I will be. Even though it's the right decision, it still sucks. I hate knowing I wasted four years of my life on someone who didn't deserve me, but whatever. You live, you learn, right?" She shrugs and releases a heavy sigh. "I'm sorry I didn't call you back this week."

I squeeze her shoulder. "It's totally fine. I get it."

"I wasn't sick—I just needed a few mental health days, aka alone time on my couch with a gallon of ice cream. Garrett thought I needed a change of scenery, so he dragged me here tonight. Naturally, I've been crying most of the evening because people keep asking where Marc is, so his plan kinda backfired. You and Dean just rescued him from another blubber fest." She forces a smile. "Anyway, enough about me. Tell me everything."

I glance at Dean, who's still engrossed in conversation with Garrett. Since he's occupied for the time being, I give her a brief rundown. I leave out our engagement news, because she does *not* need to hear about that right now.

Her eyes shine with happiness by the time I finish my story. Smiling, she wraps me in a tight hug. "I'm so excited for you, chicky. He's a great guy. I knew he'd pull his head out of his ass."

The four of us chat for a while, then load up our plates at the buffet table. After stuffing ourselves with pasta and various sides, Dean and I excuse ourselves to the dance floor. He holds me close, and I rest my head on his shoulder as we sway to the music.

"Is Lena all right?"

"She called off her engagement, so she's hurting right now, but she did the right thing. Eventually, she'll be OK."

"Did you mention anything about us?"

"Everything but our engagement." I peer up at his face. "Please don't think I'm not excited—I'm beyond happy—it just wasn't the right time for her to hear something like that."

"I understand." He kisses me. "I'm relieved you haven't changed your mind."

I pinch his ass. "Not gonna happen."

"Good. There's something I need to tell you."

I meet his gaze. "Uh, that sounds ominous."

"Don't worry, it's not." His gorgeous eyes burn into mine. "It's almost midnight. I know you wanted to ring in the new year with everyone else, but I'd love if we went someplace more private to talk."

My stomach flip flops. "Now you're really making me nervous."

He chuckles. "Relax. I already told you it wasn't anything bad."

"How about out there?" I point to the lobby.

"That works. C'mon." He loops his arm around my waist and guides me away from the crowd.

We enter the lobby and settle on a bench by a breathtaking marble fountain.

Dean takes my hand. "I, uh, told you a little lie earlier, and I've decided it's time to come clean. I wasn't late today because of traffic."

"Okaaay." I search his face, but he doesn't look the slightest bit remorseful. Nope, he's smiling from ear to ear. "So, you're pleased with yourself for being dishonest?"

He grins wider. "No. Of course not."

"You're confusing the shit out of me."

He squeezes my hand. "I know." He points to the enormous clock on a nearby wall. It's eleven fifty-seven. "We're almost there."

"You're seriously making me wait until midnight?"

"That's the plan, yes."

"Dean." I grip the front of his suit jacket. "Please tell me what's going on."

The bastard smiles and points to the clock again. "Patience, sweetheart."

"Politician," I blurt, staring up at his face.

Dean laughs. "Did you really just use your safe word because you're too impatient to wait another minute and a half?"

I lift my chin. "And what if I did?"

"You wasted your breath." He taps the tip of my nose. "It only works in the bedroom."

I narrow my eyes and release a little growl. "You're infuriating."

"And you're sexy as fuck when you're mad." He brushes his thumb over my lower lip. "Don't worry, I'll let you take out all your aggression on me later."

Finally, the first chime of midnight rings out. I peer at Dean expectantly.

"I came back to New York last night. I stayed at a hotel because I had an interview this morning. All day, actually."

"What kind of interview?"

"A job interview." He grins. "I'm happy to announce I accepted a position at New York General Hospital."

My heart leaps, and my mouth drops open. "Oh my God! You're moving here?"

"Yes, ma'am. I'm sorry I fibbed, but I didn't want to say anything in case I didn't get the job."

Tears fill my eyes. "That doesn't count as a lie. It's a surprise, and I love those. I'm so freaking happy right now."

"Me too." He cups my face. "So, I was kinda hoping you'd let me—"

"Move in with me?"

"Not what I was gonna say, but yes. I need you to be cool with that too."

"Of course I'm cool with that, silly! I can't fucking wait." I bounce in my seat, unable to contain my excitement. "Go ahead. Sorry I interrupted."

Cheers of "Happy new year" erupt from the ballroom, and the DJ plays an upbeat version of "Auld Lang Syne."

"I was hoping you'd let me start off the new year by giving you a proper proposal." Sliding off the bench, Dean sinks to one knee and pulls a ring from his pocket. "Marry me, Camille." An enormous diamond sparkles in the light as he slides the ring onto my finger. "Be mine forever."

"I've always been yours." I kiss him passionately, weaving my hands into his hair.

Time stands still, and the rest of the world disappears. He promised we'd figure it out, and he delivered. Now we can finish writing our story. Together. Our hard-won love is a gift, and the future is ours to unwrap.

THE END

Thank you for reading ***Unwrapped***.
I hope you enjoyed Cami and Dean's story!

For **Lena's** story check out ***True North***.

Curious about **The River**? Check out ***Entangled***.

ALSO BY ARIA WYATT

Compass Series
True North
North Star
Horizon

Prodigy Series
Masquerade

Standalones
Afterglow
Devil in the Details
Entangled

ABOUT THE AUTHOR

Aria Wyatt is a pharmacist mom who spends the inhumane predawn hours with a cup of coffee and her laptop, gleefully indulging in her passion for romance. Her novels range in heat from steamy to scorching, and she doesn't shy away from writing flawed characters with real life issues.

She resides with her husband and two children in New York's picturesque Hudson Valley, near the Catskills and iconic Woodstock. The avid reader balances marriage, motherhood, her pharmacist career, and her romance author dream. When not writing, she dabbles in photography, using the natural beauty of the region to her advantage. She's a self-proclaimed cat lady who cannot live without coffee, chocolate, music, and books.

Author of True North and the Compass Series, Aria has a soft spot for those who are searching, yearning, and ultimately, finding. Whether on a mission to find themselves, find love, find forgiveness or solace, she believes the answer is out there somewhere.

"Journey to Love."

Website: www.ariawyatt.com
Social media links: linktr.ee/ariawyatt
Join my readers' group on Facebook: Aria Wyatt's Speakeasy

ACKNOWLEDGEMENTS

Jen Liese, thank you for believing in me. I love you!

Thank you to **my beta reader author friends** who always give me constructive feedback and encouragement. You're all amazing and I appreciate the hell out of you.

To my cover designer, **Kate Farlow**, you're amazing. Thank you for bringing my vision to life.

To the bloggers and bookish peeps of Romancelandia, thank you for going out of your way to spread the word. I truly appreciate every one of you. I see you, **Kelly B.**, **Amy S.**, **Mikayla S.**, **Katie P.**, **Stacy C.**, **Krystal D.**, **Daria K.**, and the countless others who have taken a chance on me.

To all of **my amazing author friends**, you inspire me. Keep writing.

To my author bestie, **Kristie Wolf**, I love you, and I'm so happy to have you in my life!

Thank you to **my husband and children** for being supportive and patient with me. I love you so much.

Lastly, thank you to **my readers** for connecting with my words and characters. I couldn't do this without you!

Much love,
Aria

www.ingramcontent.com/pod-product-compliance
Lightning Source LLC
LaVergne TN
LVHW040056080526
838202LV00045B/3663